SWORD KISSED

THE DARK FAE HOLLOWS ~ HOLLOW 2

LEIGH ANDERSON

EVERSHADE
PUBLISHING

Sword Kissed Hero: The Dark Fae Hollows – Hollow 2 © 2018 Leigh Anderson

Demons of Japanese myth lurk in Chiyoko Hollow, and if they aren't stopped soon, the magic of the lands will be twisted beyond salvation.

Akari Tanaka is Sword Kissed, a human born with the power to harness magic through her katana. Her duty is to keep the residents—fae and human alike—safe from the increasingly dangerous demons that haunt Chiyoko Hollow. When people across Chiyoko begin disappearing, Akari is determined to find them—but so is half-fae warrior Takeo, who prefers to work alone.

As the bodies of the missing start turning up, drained of their life force, Akari realizes that they aren't dealing with just any twisted demon. Now her sensei is missing, her sister has been spirited away, and her childhood rival has united with a demon of smoke and ash. But with their list of enemies growing longer and their allies shorter, if Akari and Takeo can't learn to work together, the evil that threatens their world will prevail. And once that happens, there's no turning back.

Fans of J. Y. Yang and Marjorie M. Liu will be spirited away by this dystopian paranormal romance based on Japanese lore.

SWORD KISSED is a standalone contribution to the Charmed Legacy Dark Fae Hollows collection. Stories can be read in any order. *To learn more, visit CharmedLegacy.com*

1

*A*kari Tanaka braced as the impact from the katana reverberated through her body. She looked up at her opponent, Endo Ryo, and saw the smirk on her face. Akari gripped her sword and pushed up on her elbows, readying to take Endo down, but Endo's face hardened and she took another step forward.

Akari quickly rolled away as Endo swung at her. Akari flipped over and launched to her feet. She ran her sword over her hand, slicing open her flesh and causing her blade to glow with a blue aura. Her hand almost instantly healed before she was even able to tighten her grip.

Endo laughed. "What are you doing? I'm not a demon. That won't help you here."

She may have been right, but training to kill demons was Akari's job, so she preferred to treat the training sessions as realistic as possible. Besides, imagining Endo as a demon wasn't that much of a stretch of the imagination. The two had been rivals since they were girls.

The glowing sword gave Akari the confidence boost she

needed. She gritted her teeth and rubbed the ball of her foot on the mat as she prepared to attack.

"Hold," Sera calmly said as she stepped into the practice arena. Everyone except Akari lowered their swords and stepped aside. Akari grunted in frustration.

"I can do it, Sensei," Akari said as she tightened her grip even more and glared at Endo.

Sera raised her hand to silence her. "You are using far more energy than necessary. You will burn out long before your opponent will. Do not keep pushing yourself beyond what you are capable of. Learn from the experience so you will be stronger next time."

"But I can do it," Akari argued. Everyone's jaw dropped, and Sera looked at her directly. "...Sensei," she added quickly, making sure to sound respectful. "Just because I appear weak or beaten doesn't mean I am. You mustn't give up, even when it looks like you are going to lose."

Some of Akari's classmates shook their heads, shocked Akari would question the sensei's teachings. Others started to whisper among themselves. Akari felt sweat drip down her back, and not because of her exertion during the fight.

Sera smirked. "And how will you know if you have lost or if you should keep going?"

"I suppose I will know in the moment," Akari said, not relaxing her stance.

"In this moment," Sera said, turning away, "the match is at an end, as is this training session. See you all tomorrow."

Everyone gave the sensei a deep bow, and Akari finally lowered her sword, the blue glow fading. Akari did not bow as deeply as she should have. Most of the students headed for the showers from the practice arena. Endo had a pleased look on her face as she gave Akari one last glance before leaving. Akari stuffed down her anger as she stayed behind to get in a few punches with a practice dummy.

"Are you mad you lost?" her friend Kaya asked as she stood behind the dummy. "Or mad you lost to her, Akari-chan?"

Akari shot her an angry look, grunting as she slapped at the dummy's protruding prongs.

Kaya rolled her eyes and stepped away. "You never give up. Not sure if they call that tenacity or stupidity."

Akari screwed her face up as she punched and kicked at the dummy harder and faster.

"I could have beaten her," Akari finally said, out of breath. She gave the dummy one last punch in its blank face before she went over and grabbed a towel to wipe her brow.

"Then tomorrow you will," Kaya said, patting her shoulder and then making a grossed-out face as she wiped Akari's sweat from her palm.

"Thanks for the encouragement," Akari said, pulling Kaya in for a bear hug.

"Ugh! No! *Yuck*," Kaya yelled as she fought to pull away. Akari laughed as she let her go.

"Still," Kaya said. She wiped herself down and then grabbed their bottles of water. "You didn't need to light your sword. There are no demons here. Only egos as big as oni."

Akari sighed as she took a bottle from Kaya and took a big gulp. "Maybe," she said. "But what is the point of practice if we don't take it seriously?"

"We are Sword Kissed," Kaya said. "The light will always burn within us."

Sword kissed, Akari thought, rolling the title over the top of her tongue. It always sounded strange to her even though it had been her life for as long as she could remember.

The Sword Kissed were a class of warrior women with innate abilities to fight demons by virtue of their blood through their swords.

"As darkness filled the world,
the Light of one woman shone,

and thus, all were saved," as the haiku explaining the birth of the first Sword Kissed went. It also summed up how the world came to be as it was.

"Come on," Kaya said, handing Akari her sword. "Take a breath."

Kaya stood in front of a mirror, holding her sword in front of her, and took several calming breaths. Then she dipped her sword to the right, and gently moved her body with it. Swooping her sword to the left, she dipped into a crouch before rising and holding the weapon out straight while balancing on one foot.

Sword dancing was part of their training. It built strength, stamina, agility, dexterity, and grace. Kaya was a better sword dancer than Akari. When Akari faced an enemy, she preferred to charge in, her sword blazing, ready to take the demon down with as few stabs as possible. Kaya, on the other hand, was more thoughtful, methodical. She preferred to use as little of her own energy as possible, by drawing her enemy out and coaxing them into attacking her. Her methods usually took more time, but required more finesse, and usually ended up with less blood and pain.

Akari joined her sword sister in the dance. They moved as one, slowly and delicately, spinning, ducking, and weaving their blades through the air.

She tried to forget about Endo. She and Endo had been rivals since they were girls. Sera was the most sought-after sword-kissed trainer. She had originally agreed to train Endo. But after Akari was discovered, Sera took her on instead. Endo's parents were furious, but there was little they could do. It wasn't like they could refuse to allow Endo to be Sword Kissed. They had to accept the other trainer—who was quite good, but no Sera—and Endo grew into a competent Sword Kissed in her own right. She often kept Akari on her toes...on days like today and many others. Akari admitted to herself she was only as good of a fighter as she was because of Endo. But she would never admit such a thing out loud.

Akari felt the anger and stress of the day wearing off as she moved in tune with Kaya, and her movements became more fluid. She was almost sad as they came to the end of the routine.

"Thanks, Kaya," Akari said as they toweled off and prepared to head out. "That really helped."

"I'm glad," Kaya said with a smile.

As Akari turned toward the door, she was sure she saw the edge of Sera's robes disappear around the corner. Sera had been watching them. Of course she had been. Sera was always watching. But she hadn't said anything. Akari slipped out. She had no desire to talk to Sera anyway.

She exited the dojo and trotted down the front steps of the building. The dojo was part of Sera's home. The largest structure in town at six stories tall, the building was once a castle in the traditional style and was considered by many to be thousands of years old. Somehow, it had survived the Great Divide.

Legend claimed that at one time the world was one, with many continents and oceans, countries and peoples. Then a great calamity happened. No one knew what it was really, but the result was the earth was divided into thirteen Hollows, each almost separate from the others through invisible barriers no one had been able to breech. They only knew the other Hollows still existed due to occasional radio signals that would come through.

Akari lived in southern Chiyoko Hollow, which, according to history books, had once been called Japan. Legends also said the great calamity had also ripped open the world, releasing demons, fairies, hill folk, and other creatures of myth and magic into the world.

The fae were almost identical to humans, tall, rational, community-oriented beings. Except they were able to wield some forms of magic and came in a variety of colors, such as blue, orange, and pink. Some had spots or stripes or even horns or other markings. They also had pointed ears and were generally leaner, stronger, and faster than humans. Akari suspected the fae had even more powers and abilities than she was aware of, but the fae kept some things to themselves.

The fae were few in number, and humans did not trust their magical abilities. So most fae lived in small communities outside of the main cities. Their villages were usually more rustic, with thatched homes and livelihoods derived from the land. Akari knew it wasn't right the fae were forced to live apart from the rest of humanity—as her sister Yoshimi constantly reminded her— yet she tried to stay out of the discussions while doing her best to protect all people, fae and human alike.

No matter what the legends said, it was true that demons— some benign, some deadly—prowled their lives. And it was the responsibility of the Sword Kissed to keep the monsters at bay. In the past, the job had not been too difficult because everyone knew the creatures and how to avoid the dangerous ones. Over the years, though, there had been a change. The creatures, all of them, were becoming more aggressive and unpredictable. Akari never knew when she might be called upon to take down a murdering basan or trap and release a troublesome nobusuma.

Akari wandered through the marketplace, trying to figure out what to fix for dinner. She wasn't in much of a hurry since she knew Yoshimi wouldn't be home from classes for another hour. She picked out a nice fresh fish that would be delicious grilled and a few vegetables she could steam as she cooked rice. She was haggling with a seller over the price of some fresh berries when she heard raised voices.

"Hey! Look out," someone yelled.

She looked up just as a small hooded creature crashed into her, knocking her to the ground and spilling her purchases in the dirt. Grunting, she made her way back to her feet and gave chase. She couldn't believe she let someone catch her off guard! She felt her anger rise, which helped her run faster. In only a moment, she was able to grab the small creature by the collar and turn it around. She was surprised to see she'd caught a small fae child.

"What's wrong with you?" she asked, shaking him slightly. "What are you doing?"

The child, who was blue-tinged and had pointed ears, shook in fear and clutched something in his hands.

"What do you have there?" she asked. "What did you steal?"

He tried to keep a tight hold of it, but Akari grabbed his arm. He dropped two steamed buns. They would have been quite cheap to purchase.

"Where are your parents?" she asked. The little boy shook his head. "What do you mean? Speak up."

"Dead," he finally whispered.

"What?" she asked, loosening her grip. "How?"

The boy shook his head again. The shopkeeper who had originally called out finally came up behind Akari.

"Good job, Tanaka-san," he said. "Now we can teach this thief a lesson." He tried to grab the boy away from her, but she placed herself between him and the child.

The shopkeeper, like everyone else in the immediate area, was human. She knew he would be more motivated by his hate of fae than of losing two steamed buns.

"I'll handle this," she said. She started to drag the boy away.

"What about me?" the shopkeeper asked. "How am I to be compensated?"

"You can have the fish I dropped," she said. "I'm sure it's still flopping on the street somewhere."

The man grunted. "Fae-lover," he scowled under his breath.

Akari ignored him, heading back to the dojo. Sera was not only the main Sword Kissed trainer, but their commander as well. She needed to tell Sera what happened and ask her how she wanted her to proceed.

She noticed as they left the market that the boy looked back longingly and licked his lips. She stopped by a different stall and bought him two steamed buns, which he devoured in a couple of bites.

"Calm down, kid," she said. "You are going to make yourself sick. How long has it been since you've eaten?"

He just shrugged.

"Where are you from?" she asked.

"Ryu," he said, which was the capital city. What was a fae child from Ryu doing here without parents? Compared to Ryu, the city of Nasu was nothing but a backwater burg.

They entered Sera's home and were shown into the main reception area. "It doesn't make sense," Akari said to Sera.

Sera kneeled in front of the boy and smiled at him. "Why don't you head over there and feed the fish?" she said, motioning toward a koi pond out in the front garden. The boy nodded, exiting to wander over to the pond. Akari and Sera moved to the porch and watched him as they spoke.

"Fae don't have orphans," Sera said when the boy was out of earshot. "They take care of their own. If his parents were killed somehow, another fae family would have taken him in."

"Yet, not only did they not take him in," Akari mused, "he somehow made his way here, all alone."

Sera nodded. "I have contacts in Ryu. I'll find out what they know. Dead fae and missing kids won't go unnoticed. Someone will know something."

The kid dropped some small pieces of food into the pond and watched the fish, but there was no joy on his face. He seemed distant, haunted.

"What are you going to do with him for now?" Akari asked. Nasu was mostly made up of humans, so no one was going to go out of their way to take care of the kid.

"I'm not sure," Sera said. "We aren't really set up to be a daycare."

"Have you sent for Yoshimi?" Akari asked. "She might have an idea."

"What might I have an idea about?" Yoshimi asked. She entered the gate and walked up the path. Once she reached the porch, she gave Sera a bow.

Akari smirked and shot a look to Sera. Of course she had already sent for Yoshimi. Sera was not the sort of person to leave anything to chance. Akari nodded toward the kid. "What to do with him," she said. "I found him stealing in the marketplace."

"Does he have some horrifying plague?" Yoshimi asked.

"Umm...no..." Akari said.

"Then why is he out there all alone? He must be terrified," Yoshimi said. Shooting them a reproachful look, she went over and squatted down next to him.

Akari watched as Yoshimi talked to the boy for only a moment, helped him feed the fish, and then took him lovingly in her arms. Yoshimi was good with kids, a teacher, and had a kind heart, unlike Akari. Akari had no patience with kids. Or people in general. She had few friends and even fewer social graces. While she didn't feel the need to be more gentle, she admired Yoshimi's nurturing bearing.

After a moment, Yoshimi took the boy by the hand and they walked over to Akari and Sera.

"He's coming home with us," Yoshimi declared. "Elwin-chan, why don't you go over there and pick some plums to take home with us?" she said. She motioned to a plum tree across the yard. The boy nodded and ran over to the tree, carefully examining each plum, looking for the best one.

"Elwin?" Akari asked.

"Yes, his name is Elwin," Yoshimi said. "Didn't you bother asking?" Akari shrugged her shoulders while Yoshimi rolled her eyes. "The child has been through a terrible trauma. His parents killed, on the run alone, starving. Have a little compassion."

"But why is he on the run?" Akari asked. "That's what is important here."

"What's important here is a little scared kid," Yoshimi said firmly. "We can find out more details later. Right now, he needs safety and comfort if we want him to talk."

"I agree," Sera said. "Take him home, ladies. See what you can find out. I'll do what I can from here." As they turned to leave, Sera called out to Akari. "Tanaka-san," she said. "Stay a moment."

"We don't have anything to eat at home," Akari said to Yoshimi. "He made me drop my fish."

Yoshimi nodded and took Elwin by the hand. "We will find something. Won't we, buddy?" she asked him with a big smile. The boy timidly smiled back.

After they were gone, Akari turned back to Sera and waited for her chastisement.

"Have you given any more thought to our training session today?" Sera asked.

"Not really," Akari said, crossing her arms. "I could have beaten her."

"That's not the point," Sera said. "You are a good fighter, and I know you want to protect the town. But I can't promote you if you don't listen to me."

"Oh, come on," Akari exclaimed, a bit too loudly. "That's crap, and you know it. You just said you wanted to promote me. I've more than proven my skill, my worth."

"Training never ends, Akari," Sera said, walking over to the pond. She pulled out a long reed, and she used it to rearrange the lily pads floating along the water. Akari had no idea how old Sera was. She was a fixture in the town. Everyone knew who she was and respected her. She had the bearing of an old woman, but her hair was still full and black, and she had few wrinkles. When she was a child, she assumed Sera was simply timeless, like a goddess sent from the stars to train her. As an adult, Akari knew better, but still not enough about her mentor.

"Even if I promote you," Sera continued after she was satisfied with the lily pad placement, "you will need to listen to me and work together with your fellow Sword Kissed. I think you would see a promotion as...an ending. Just a final goal. You are Sword Kissed for life. It won't ever end."

Akari nearly shuddered, but she forced herself to still. The thought of being Sword Kissed for her entire life, for fighting monsters to never end, to one day only moving from killing demons to training more Sword Kissed filled her with dread, boredom, and hopelessness.

This wasn't the life she wanted.

"I know," was all she finally managed to say. How else could she reply? She had a job, a duty to uphold. As much as she might loathe it, there was nothing else for her.

"Good," Sera said, but Akari had a feeling Sera knew she was holding back. But Akari did not want to wait around and carry on with the conversation. She gave Sera a low bow before exiting the complex as quickly as possible.

That evening, Akari tried not to think about what Sera had said. She focused her energy on the little fae boy staying in her house.

Akari, Elwin, and Yoshimi all sat around the low dining table on the tatami mats together to eat chicken with plum sauce Yoshimi had cooked up. The boy was quiet, but occasionally, he and Yoshimi shared a knowing glance and giggle. They had apparently already bonded quite a bit while Akari was detained.

After Yoshimi put the boy to bed, the sisters sat together in the living room with a couple of cups of sake.

"Did anyone give you any trouble on the way home?" Akari

asked. She held her cup to her nose and breathed in the sweet aroma.

"Just some dirty looks," Yoshimi said. She sipped at her drink. "But nothing I wouldn't expect."

Akari downed her drink in one gulp. "Has he told you anything yet? Anything useful?"

"It will take time for him to learn to trust me—" Yoshimi started to explain, but Akari cut her off.

"We might not have a lot of time," she said. "This is a dangerous situation. You know the people around here will not be accepting of—"

"Of a child?" Yoshimi asked, interrupting Akari. Akari rolled her eyes. He wasn't just a child, even if Yoshimi wanted to pretend otherwise. "You are just as prejudiced against the fae as anyone, even if you think otherwise."

"I'm just trying to protect him, and the rest of the fae in this town," Akari said.

"By keeping them separate?" Yoshimi asked, her annoyance rising, as was typical when she got on the subject of how the fae were treated. "By treating them like they don't belong?"

"If keeping them separate keeps them safe," Akari said, pouring herself another cup. She moved to refill Yoshimi's cup as well, but Yoshimi put her cup on a side table out of Akari's reach. "Then yes, I will keep them separate."

"You aren't fixing the problems around here," Yoshimi said, crossing her arms. "You are just delaying them."

"We can't all devote our lives to the fae," Akari said, more sharply than she intended.

"Teaching at a fae school doesn't mean I have devoted my lives to them," Yoshimi said. "If the fae children were allowed to attend the same school as humans, I would teach there."

"You know what happened the last time we tried admitting fae kids," Akari said.

"Do we?" Yoshimi asked. "That was before either of us were

born. And how come the answer was sending the fae to their own school instead of punishing those humans who rioted? The problem was only delayed, not fixed. The fae children should have been allowed to stay in the school back then."

Akari poured herself another cup of sake even though her cheeks were already hot. Yoshimi was probably right. But what could Akari do about it now?

"I'm doing my best here, nii-chan," Akari said, using the endearing term for *older sister* to let her know she wasn't angry. "I could use your support."

Yoshimi sighed. "That little boy needs our support. You are a grown woman, imōuto. If you don't take a stand on this issue soon, you are only going to fall."

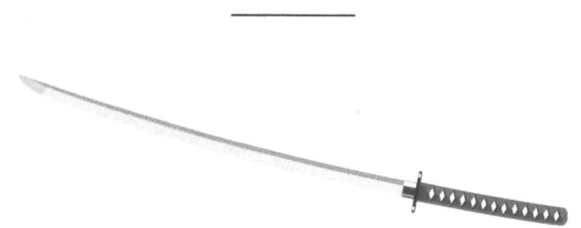

2

"What have you learned?" Sera asked Akari the next day. Akari had arrived early, before the day's training session. Yoshimi often awoke and headed to the school long before Akari woke up. So she had risen with her sister with the hopes of speaking to Elwin again, but he had not been any less tight-lipped than the day before. He ate as though he was still ravenous and then eagerly followed Yoshimi out the door. He was probably anxious to be around fellow fae again.

"Not much, Sensei," Akari said. "Elwin still isn't talking, but Yoshimi is taking him to the fae school today. She is hoping the other children can help draw him out, or the fae parents."

Sera nodded. "That is a good plan. If the Ryu fae don't take him back, we may need to find him a more permanent situation here."

"Anything else?" Akari asked hopefully, not in the mood to face Endo in the dojo today. She hoped Sera knew of some demons in the area for her to track down, so she wouldn't have to head to practice.

"What do you know about zashiki-warashi?" Sera asked her.

"A good fortune child?" Akari asked. "Usually a rather benign creature. Said to bestow gifts on people who manage to see one. Why? What about it?"

"One has been seen near Kuji, one of the fae villages," Sera explained. Akari knew the village well. It was the one Yoshimi taught at. "Only it isn't giving out good fortune. A well has been poisoned, and several goats have been killed."

Akari nodded and gripped the handle of her katana, which hung at her side. "I will handle it. Will Kaya be going with me?" The Sword Kissed were usually sent in pairs.

"The village elder asked for you specifically, and only you," Sera said. Akari gave a knowing nod. The village would have wanted as few outsiders in the village as possible. At least Akari was somewhat known to them.

"Be careful," Sera said. "And not just of the zashiki-warashi."

Akari understood her meaning as she headed out to Kuji. As much as humans distrusted fae, the fae trusted humans even less in this area. And with just cause. The humans had not dealt fairly with the fae over the years, she had to admit.

As Akari rode her horse into Kuji, she was met with the suspicious glares she expected, but no one said anything to her. Even though her sister was accepted by the fae community, Akari was not. The community was generally considered to be a safe and happy place. They didn't have their own protection force because they rarely needed it. They had village elders who generally were enough to keep the community running smoothly. As Akari rode to the main community hut, she was met by one of the elders.

He greeted her with a bow. "Tanaka-san," he said. "Welcome. I am Aimon Naeran." He was so old his hair had gone almost completely white. His skin had an orange tinge to it, and he had many wrinkles.

She was surprised and not that Yoshimi was not there as well. After all, Yoshimi was her "in" with the local populous, but Yoshimi had a job to do as well. The village elder probably thought if he appeared to need Yoshimi as an intermediary, he might lose face, as though he was incapable of dealing with Akari himself.

She smiled and gave him a respectful bow. "Naeran-san. Thank you for your warm greeting. I just wish it had been under better circumstances."

He motioned for her to follow him into the large hut. Inside, the room was warm, with large braziers burning. The smoke wafted gently out of an opening in the ceiling.

"When the well was poisoned," he explained, "the people were not scared, but angry. They thought the humans were to blame."

Akari nodded and crossed her arms, looking around the room. There were several elderly women present, weaving baskets or laying out tea leaves to dry. This seemed to be a workspace for more elderly residents since the room was warm and dry. "I can understand why that would be their first suspicion."

"But then, I learned a zashiki-warashi had been seen in an old abandoned barn in the woods," he explained as he sat down. "Tea?" he asked. He didn't wait for her to answer before motioning for a servant girl, a pretty little thing with violet coloring but the longest ears Akari had ever seen, to bring a tea tray. Akari obliged and sat on her knees in front of Lord Naeran.

"Who saw the creature?" she asked.

"Some children who were playing where they shouldn't," he said. "But then my son, Galan, went to investigate and saw the creature. That night, four of his goats died. Four! That is more than bad luck."

Akari nodded. That was a serious loss for a small community. "And you are sure it was a zashiki-warashi?" she asked as she fidgeted with her teacup. "A well poisoning or dead goats could have a mundane cause. You are sure it was not one of your own people, or an outsider? You haven't seen anyone new lurking around, have you?"

"Believe me, Tanaka-san," he said, "the last thing we want are humans traipsing through our community causing us more problems."

Akari bristled a little at that, but she tried not to let it show.

"We examined every possible explanation," he said. "But it was certainly a zashiki-warashi. I finally saw it myself last night. We would not have sent for you otherwise."

Akari nodded. She knew he was right; they would have only sent for a Sword Kissed as a last resort.

"Point me toward the barn," she said, standing.

Lord Naeran took her outside and pointed the way. She nodded her thanks and tried to give the people who were watching her a smile, but they did not respond in kind.

There was a trail leading into the woods and up a hill. Akari took a moment to look out over the village below and take in the beauty of the area. The trees were sprouting with new growth, and a slight breeze in the air tickled the hairs on her arms. It was early spring and the sakura—cherry—blossoms were just begging to bud. They would start falling soon. She took a deep breath and continued toward the barn.

The trees were thick here, so even in the brightest part of the day, it was gloomy the deeper into the forest she moved. She moved carefully and silently, not stepping on any branches or fallen leaves.

"Sakura, sakura..."

She gasped as she heard a small voice singing a familiar tune. One her mother sang to her when she was a child.

"Blossoms on the trees,
Blossoms in the sky.
Are you a human,
Or are you a fairy?
Sakura, sakura of mine..."

She followed the sound of the voice, and then peeked into the barn through a crack in the wood.

"Sakura...sakura..."

She saw what from behind looked like a small child with bobbed hair. The child raised its hand, and she saw it had reddish skin. Definitely a zashiki-warashi. She leaned back and looked left and right, wondering which path would be better to take. But when she peered back through the crack, the zashiki-warashi was gone.

"Crap," she whispered. She went around the side of the barn and nearly shrieked.

She found herself face to face with a furry red beast. The large beast bared its fangs and drool dripped down.

"Sakura..." the beast growled. "Sakura..."

"Leave this place," Akari warned as she drew her sword. "Or I will have no choice but to vanquish you." She was feigning courage. She had never known a zashiki-warashi to take on such a hideous form. What was wrong with it? What else was it capable of besides the bad luck it had already caused?

The beast let out what sounded like a low, grumbling laugh. "You cannot stop me," it said. "Our time has come."

It then zipped away from her, impossibly fast for its size. Akari lunged after it, but she quickly lost sight of it.

"Come back, beast," she called. "Face me!"

"As you wish," another voice, this one clearer and more feminine, said. Was there someone else in the woods? Was she facing more than one enemy? Akari raised her sword and turned in a slow circle, keeping her eyes wide for any movement.

The beast then let out a horrid scream as it burst through some undergrowth and ran toward her at full speed. Akari held her sword aloft, planning to run the creature through as it attacked, but the creature, with its bare hands, batted her sword out of the way and knocked her to the ground easily. Too easily.

She didn't come prepared for this. A zashiki-warashi was

usually a small, gentle creature. Even if it was doing naughty, mischievous things, she couldn't understand why it would have taken on such a monstrous form. What had caused the change? How was she to defeat it?

She scrambled back to her feet, grabbed her sword, and ducked behind a tree as the creature tried to pummel her.

Akari came from around the tree, swinging her sword at the creature's ankle. She sliced through the fur and skin, and it screamed again as it fell. But Akari did not let her guard down, for she knew a wounded animal could be even more dangerous than it had been. She stood back, out of the beast's reach.

"You can stop this," Akari said. "I don't need to kill you. Retake your true form and stop cursing the villagers."

The monster laughed again. "Are you a human, or are you a fairy? Sweet sakura of mine," the creature sang in its terrifying growl. Then it laughed again.

"This is your last warning," Akari said, raising her sword.

The beast shrieked again and lunged at her, swiping at her with its large paws and claws.

Akari stepped back and then swung her sword to the left, the right. She feigned a step back, but then moved forward, spinning around behind the creature and slicing it along the back. The beast fell forward with a pained cry.

"Do you yield?" she asked.

It looked back at her. "Never, sakura of mine..." It shrieked as it lunged. Akari stepped to the side but held her sword out, impaling the creature. She felt its body go limp, and she kicked it backward off her sword. It fell to the ground, black blood, like tar, seeping from it. The ichor was absorbed into the dirt.

"What the hell?" she asked aloud. As far as she knew, all magical creatures bled green blood. Even the fae. She also noticed the plants seemed to recoil away from the dead beast. Magical beings were born of the earth. When they died, they were usually reclaimed by the earth in an embrace of ivy, bugs, and flowers. But the ground around this creature turned as black as its blood as the plants pulled away.

"What happened?" a woman behind her asked. Akari turned and saw the servant who had poured her tea earlier.

"I had to kill it," Akari said. "It had transformed into a dangerous beast. But look at the blood. It's as if the creature was infected. I need to speak to Lord Naeran about this."

"That is why I came to find you, Tanaka-san," the maid said. "Naeran-san...he is gone."

"What do you mean he is gone?" Akari asked, standing.

"Just that," the maid said, her hands shaking and her eyes brimming with tears. "He told me to fetch his writing kit, and when I returned, he was gone. I have looked everywhere."

"This doesn't make any sense," Akari said under her breath. She looked around the woods one more time. There had been another voice, the voice of a woman earlier. What had happened to her? Was she still here? Had she fled when she saw that the zashiki-warashi was no match for Akari's skills? She listened, hoping to hear the fluttering of leaves or the crushing of twigs underfoot, but there was nothing. Whoever else had been here was gone now.

Akari walked quickly back to the village, the maid on her heels. A young man who looked similar to Lord Naeran approached Akari as soon as she returned.

"Is it over?" he asked. "Did you get rid of the zashiki-warashi?"

"Are you Naeran-san's son, Galen?" she asked. "The one who lost the goats?"

"I am," he said with a hint of pride.

"Where is your father? I must speak with him."

"If he is not with the other village elders, then I assume he is in his home," he said. "Come."

They went past the main community hut they had been in earlier to a large home nearby.

"Otōsan?" the young man called, banging on the door. "Otōsan, the Sword Kissed has vanquished the zashiki-warashi. Come and thank her."

But there was no reply. Glancing back, Akari saw the maid who had found her in the woods was standing there, her head bowed.

"I'm sorry, my lord," the maid said, her trembling apparent as the tips of her ears fluttered. "But I have looked everywhere. I cannot find him."

"What could have happened?" Galen asked.

"Your father, I think he mentioned seeing the zashiki-warashi," Akari asked.

"He did," Galen replied. "The day after the goats died, he went to investigate. He said he couldn't send for the Sword Kissed without confirming the presence of the zashiki-warashi."

Akari shook her head. "Anyone who sees a zashiki-warashi is given a blessing," she said. "Or in the case of this...mutated creature, a curse."

"After the village children saw it," Galen said with a nod. "The well was poisoned. After I saw it, my goats died."

"Maybe after your father saw it," Akari said, "he was cursed to disappear."

"What about you?" he asked. "You saw it as well."

"But I killed it," she said. "It can't curse me if it is dead."

"But my father..." he said, shaking his head disbelievingly, the truth of the matter seemingly sinking in. He swayed a bit, and the maid helped keep him from collapsing. "He is gone?"

"I'm so sorry," Akari said, and meant it.

"*No*," Galen cried out. "This cannot be!" He buried his head in his hands and started to weep.

Akari darted her eyes around, realizing many of the villagers were also crying.

"What are we to do?" someone cried out.

"What if another creature comes for us?"

"Do not worry," Akari said. "The Sword Kissed will keep you safe."

The whole crowd grew silent. She had a feeling they did not want to contradict her since she had just killed the zashiki-warashi. But killing one monster was not insurance the rest of the Sword Kissed—a group of humans—would continue to keep them safe.

"When I was in the woods," Akari said, "I am sure there was someone else there. I heard another voice. I know there is something unnatural happening here. I will return, and I will protect you and your people. I give you my word."

Galen stood up and gave Akari a small bow. "I look forward to seeing the strength of your word," he said. After heading into his father's house, he shut the door.

One by one, the rest of the villagers shook their heads in disbelief and returned to their own homes.

Akari got on her horse and headed back to Nasu. Something was wrong here. She only hoped Sera would agree with her and would give her the support she needed to keep her promise to the people of Kuji.

3

"Sakura, sakura
Blossoms on the trees
Blossoms in the sky
Are you a human
Or are you a fairy?
Sakura, sakura of mine..."

*A*kari couldn't help but hum the comforting tune as she rode back to town.

"Why...why are you singing that?" Yoshimi asked.

Akari had hung around Kuji, patrolling the woods and helping them strengthen some of their outer defenses until Yoshimi got done with class. Yoshimi and Elwin were riding on their own horse. Both horses were walking slowly. They should have been home quickly since it was only a ten-minute ride to Nasu from Kuji, but neither Tanaka seemed in a hurry to get home. Yoshimi was clearly distraught over the death of Lord Naeran. He had been one of her largest supporters. He'd given her much encouragement to continue working with him on improving relations between the fae and the humans. She was certainly grieving his death, but also concerned for her future in Kuji as well.

Even though Akari was upset over the loss of Lord Naeran, the words from the song the creature sang played over and over in her head.

"So I'm not crazy," Akari said. "It is the same song?"

"Of course it is," Yoshimi nearly snapped. "I could never forget..." She sighed and turned back to the road with a shake of her head.

Their mother had died only a few years before. Akari was nearly an adult at the time, seventeen, and Yoshimi was away at college. Yet, their mother still sang the song to her before she went to sleep. Of course, she no longer tucked her daughter into bed at a certain time. Akari had put an end to that when she was thirteen, saying she didn't need to be treated like a baby anymore. Her mother agreed, yet she always stayed up in another room as long as Akari was awake. And as soon as Akari turned out her light, she could hear her mother sing the song in a whispered voice. She didn't know if her mother sang the song to help Akari go to sleep or only to comfort herself as her daughters grew up, but Akari never tried to stop her from singing. After her mother's death, she couldn't fall asleep on her own for months.

"The creature," Akari said in nearly a whisper. "It was singing the song."

"What?" Yoshimi asked. "How is that possible?"

"That's what I am wondering," Akari said. "Zashiki-warashi are known to sing folk songs to entice people to follow them, but why that particular song? It isn't a common folk tune." Akari assumed it was one her mother had made up. Did the creature somehow know the song held special meaning for Akari? It wasn't possible, but who knew all the magical ways of demons?

Akari shook her head and decided it was simply dumb luck that caused the creature to sing that song to her.

"Sakura, sakura," Elwin started to sing. He clung to Yoshimi, the side of his face resting against her back.

Akari shot him a look. "Why are you singing that song? Do you know it?"

He gasped and looked away.

"He's probably just mimicking you," Yoshimi said. "It's a pretty song."

Akari nodded, and they rode the rest of the way in uncomfortable silence. When they arrived back at Nasu, they came to their home quickly, since it was on that side of town.

"Go on home," Akari said. "I need to let Sera know what happened."

Yoshimi nodded, but didn't reply. Something was bothering her, but Akari couldn't put her finger on what. She would have to try to talk to her about it, if it didn't lead to a fight. Like all sisters, Akari and Yoshimi loved each other, but they had their disagreements and shared history they would rather not talk about.

"What happened out there?" Sera asked as soon as Akari returned.

"The creature," Akari said. With a sigh, she fixed herself a cup of tea to calm her nerves. "It was a zashiki-warashi; at least, it appeared to be one at first. But something was wrong with it. It's as though the creature was infected with something. It turned into a monstrous beast and attacked me. When I killed it, its black blood seeped into the earth and the plants pulled away."

Sera put her hand to her mouth, which was pinched with worry. "Anything else?"

"The village elder, Lord Naeran," Akari said solemnly. "He vanished before I could subdue the creature."

"What do you mean he vanished?" Sera asked.

"Just as I said," Akari explained. "He was there when I arrived, but when I returned to the village after fighting the creature, he was gone. I think the zashiki-warashi placed a curse on him."

"Maybe, maybe not," Sera said. She walked over and opened a door, waving someone in.

"Akari Tanaka, this is Takeo Torgwyn," she said when a tall somber man entered the room.

He was clearly fae, with his pointed ears and lithe build, but he was unlike any she had met before. His skin tone and facial features appeared completely human. Then she considered his name: Takeo Torgwyn. He had a human first name but a fae surname. She had heard that in some places, like Ryu, fae and human pairings were more accepted, but here in her more rural town of Nasu, she had never met such a couple.

"I wish we could have met under better circumstances, Tanaka-san," Takeo said. He bowed to Akari, and she awkwardly returned the gesture, not taking her eyes off his entrancing face.

His features were angular and his eyes piercing. His hair was very long. It was bound on the top of his head, but the tail flowed freely down his back. He wore a black jacket embroidered with blue in the traditional style, armed with a bow and quiver of arrows slung over his back. He also had two daggers at his sides. So not a swordsman, she surmised.

"Torgwyn-san is from Ryu," Sera said, forcing Akari to look at her. "As soon as my contacts heard about the lost fae boy and the zashiki-warashi, they sent Takeo instead of just a message."

"We had not been looking for the boy," Takeo said. "His parents disappeared weeks ago, so we thought he had vanished as well."

"If they had gone missing, shouldn't you have been looking for them?" Akari asked, crossing her arms.

Takeo cleared his throat. "Forgive me for being unclear. They did not go missing. They vanished. One moment they were there, and the next, they were not."

"It sounds like what happened with Lord Naeran," Sera said, and Akari nodded her agreement.

"Their bodies turned up just a few days ago, shriveled and the eyes black, as though their life force had been drained," Takeo explained. "The boy was nowhere to be found, so we assumed the worst. Either the boy did not vanish and instead fled here, or he was taken as well and perhaps escaped, turning up here. Either way, I need to speak to him. Then I must return him to the Ryu fae community."

"So they are all fae," Akari asked. "The boy's parents and Lord Naeran, they are all fae. Have there been more missing fae?"

Sera walked over to a table. She picked up several pieces of paper and handed them to Akari. "Torgwyn-san has been collecting these from villages around Chiyoko."

The papers were all missing persons posters. The people were fae and human, old and young, men and women. The descriptions also all used the same word to describe the disappearance—*vanished*.

"There must be half a dozen missing persons fliers here," Akari said, stunned.

Sera nodded. "But from all over Chiyiko, so no one thought they were connected until Torgwyn-san started investigating it."

"I have been looking into missing persons cases for months," Takeo said, reaching for the stack. Akari handed it to him. She wondered why he was so interested in the missing. "Of course, there are mundane causes behind disappearances all the time, but these are the ones I have found that seem to have no explanation."

"And now you can add Lord Naeran to that list as well," Akari said.

"I will," he said with a small bow. "Thank you for your assistance."

"So, what now?" Akari asked Sera. "It is possible infected zashiki-warashi are behind all the missing people? I think we should try to track them down. There could be a whole tribe of them."

Sera cleared her throat. "I would like you to work with Torgwyn-san to try and find out what is going on."

Akari shot a glance to Takeo, but his emotionless face revealed nothing. "Are you serious?" she asked. "A Sword Kissed working with a fae? In this town—"

"It is exactly what we need," Sera interrupted with a note of finality. "The divisions between the humans and fae need to be dealt with. And the Sword Kissed should set an example."

Akari wasn't so sure about that. After all, there were no fae Sword Kissed. That was not a division created out of prejudice— it was natural. Akari wanted to protest. Working with a fae could hamper her search for answers. The humans wouldn't trust Takeo while the fae would distrust Akari. But she knew better than to argue with her teacher.

"Whatever you say, Sensei," she said with a curt bow. She then turned to Takeo. "Follow me, I guess." As she walked away, she didn't hear him following her, so she stopped. When she turned back, she found her nose pressed against his chest. She quickly stepped back. "Sorry," she said. "I didn't hear you."

"Forgive me," he said. "I am used to walking silently."

His cool, impassive nature unnerved her. She couldn't tell if he wanted to work with her or not. He seemed like the type to just follow orders no matter what.

"So where do you want to start?" Akari asked. They exited the building and headed toward the street. As she expected, as soon as Takeo appeared, the people started staring. Then their stares turned to her as he spoke to her.

"I would like to see the boy," he said. "I have questions for him, and I would like to have him sent back to his people as soon as possible."

Akari nodded. "He is at my house," she said. "You can follow me."

"At *your* house?" he asked. "You have a fae community here, do you not?"

"We do," she said. "But none of the fae are connected to the Sword Kissed. My sister teaches at the fae school. She volunteered to take him in until we figured out what was going on."

Out of the corner of her eye, Akari saw him press his lips into a disapproving line.

"What?" she asked.

"Nothing," he said, staring straight ahead.

It was clear something was bothering him about the arrangement, but she wasn't going to force him to tell her. If they were going to work together, they were going to have to be civil to one another.

They arrived at Akari's home just as Yoshimi was filling bowls of rice. Yoshimi froze when she saw Takeo, her rice ladle in midair.

Elwin jumped up from his place on the tatami and ran to Takeo. It seemed to take all his resolve not to throw himself in to the elder fae's arms.

Takeo kneeled to Elwin's level and said something to him in faeish, to which Elwin excitedly replied.

Akari locked eyes with Yoshimi, asking her in their silent sister language if she understood them. Yoshimi gave a small smile in acknowledgement. She then filled two more bowls of rice and placed them around the table. Elwin took Takeo by the hand, leading him to the seat next to him. Takeo bowed to Yoshimi before sitting.

"I hate to impose, Tanaka-san," he said to her.

"Please," she replied with a bow. She waved her hand, inviting him to sit. "I only wish I had more to offer than this disgusting meal."

"I am sure it is delicious," he said, taking his seat. Elwin scooted over, sitting so close to Takeo he was practically leaning against him as he ate.

"You can call me Yoshimi," Yoshimi said, filling more bowls with miso soup.

"I am Takeo Torgwyn, Yoshimi-san," Takeo replied. "From Ryu, sent to help Sword Kissed Tanaka find some missing people."

"And find out what has cursed the zashiki-warashi in the area," Akari added, reaching to take a bowl of soup from Yoshimi.

"Yes, tell me more about this zashiki-warashi?" Takeo said.

"The one I fought today..." Akari started to explain, but she couldn't help but shudder at the experience. She picked at her fish with her chopsticks. "It was...not right. Bestial. Violent. Then it caused a fae village elder to vanish."

Elwin's eyes grew big, and he shrank next to Takeo. Yoshimi shot her sister a look of annoyance.

"Don't worry, Elwin-chan," Yoshimi cooed. "You are safe here."

"Thank you for taking the boy in," Takeo said to Yoshimi. "I heard you teach at a fae school in the area."

Yoshimi filled a small cup with sake for Takeo. "I do," she said with a small smile. "I was very happy to help the boy in any way I could."

"When I leave," Takeo said, patting the boy on the arm, "I will take Elwin with me. Find a fae family in Ryu to raise him."

Yoshimi gave him a nod and tight smile before replying, "I am sure that is for the best."

Akari wondered just how attached to the child Yoshimi had grown in only a day. Yoshimi loved children, and desperately wanted some of her own, but she had difficulty finding a husband. Not many in town approved of her constant association with the fae. And even though the fae accepted her, none of the fae men had attempted to court her—not that Akari knew of. Even if one did, she was not sure Yoshimi would accept. She had asked Yoshimi in the past if she was interested in fae men, but she only shrugged and changed the conversation, so Akari had not brought it up again.

"Perhaps we could even find a fae family here to take him in in the meantime," Takeo said with a smile at the boy. "I have no idea how long the investigation will take, so it would be good to place him with his own people while he waits."

Akari could almost feel Yoshimi's heart drop. She studied her sister's face, seeing the fear and pain there.

"The boy is fine here," Akari said to Takeo. "There is no need to move him."

"Did you ask the boy what he wants?" Takeo asked. "Or did you simply take it upon yourself to keep him like a lost puppy?"

Yoshimi let out a gasp mixed with a choke, and she put her hand to her mouth.

"My sister did what she thought was best—" Akari started to say, but Takeo interjected.

"And now that some time has passed for reflection, I am sure she can see that placing the boy with his own people would be for the best."

Yoshimi's eyes were wide in shock, and Akari's face grew hot with anger.

"How do you know what is best for him?" Akari asked. "You just come into our home and insult the kind heart of my sister?"

"I am not insulting Yoshimi-san," he said, giving Yoshimi a wan smile. "I am sure she is a good person. But we must do what is best for the child."

"How *dare* you?" Akari said, slamming down her teacup, but Yoshimi placed her hand on her sister's arm.

"Thank you for defending me, imōuto," she said. Then she turned to Takeo. "You are right I did not ask Elwin what he wanted. He was scared and alone, and the Sword Kissed didn't know what to do with him. Sera-san asked for my assistance, so I opened my home and my heart to him. You would find few humans in this town willing to do the same." She paused for a breath, and Takeo gave her a small, thankful bow of his head. "But *you* have not asked the boy what he wants either," Yoshimi continued, and Akari felt a small swell of pride in her chest at the way she called out Takeo's hypocrisy. "I would not want to submit him to more trauma by moving him again if it was not what he wanted. Please, ask him what he would like to do."

Takeo nodded and turned to Elwin. He spoke to the boy in faeish, and the boy glanced at Yoshimi before responding. Akari did not know what they said, but she could read the look of triumph on Yoshimi's face when he was done speaking.

"It looks like the boy would prefer to stay here until we return to Ryu," he said. "As long as he can continue attending the fae school."

Yoshimi ladled some pickled vegetables onto everyone's plates. "He did love going to the school today," she said. "He missed playing so freely. The children were happy to have a new playmate as well. He told me he has been very frightened ever since he fled home."

"And why did he flee home?" Akari asked. Taking a bite, she savored the sourness of the vegetables.

"Is it okay if I tell Akari and Takeo what you told me?" Yoshimi asked Elwin. He gave a small nod. Yoshimi turned back to Akari. "He said there was a monster in his home. It took his okāsan and otōusan. It was coming for him, but he got away."

"What did it look like? Was it red and hairy?" Akari asked Elwin, expecting the monster to look like the infected zashiki-warashi she saw that day.

The little boy shook his head. "Shadow," he whispered. He gazed around, as if afraid the creature would suddenly appear and whisk him away. He whimpered and nuzzled against Takeo.

"Shadow?" Akari asked. "Can you explain?"

Elwin started to cry, hiding his face in his hands. Yoshimi held her arms out, and he crawled on his knees to her. She shushed him as she took him from the room.

Akari tapped her chopsticks on the side of her bowl, considering what he said. A shadow? The zashiki-warashi she saw today definitely could not be mistaken for that.

"What do you make of that?" Takeo asked as he finished his food. "It doesn't sound like what you described."

"I'm not sure," Akari said, chewing on the end of her chopstick. "Maybe the infected zashiki-warashi can take on many frightening forms."

Takeo nodded. "That is possible. There is no telling what such dark magic can do. But there is a more worrisome possibility."

"What is that?" she asked.

"That what took the boy's parents was not a zashiki-warashi," he said.

"What sort of magical creature takes on the appearance of a shadow?" Akari wondered.

Takeo shook his head. "There are dark, twisted creatures, but none I would describe as a shadow."

Akari nodded in agreement. "I was thinking the same thing. But if the zashiki-warashi was able to take on a different form, then the shadow creature could be anything."

Takeo leaned back and sighed. "You are right. We have no idea what we are looking for."

Akari mulled this over in her head. She cleared away the dishes, taking them to the sink. Takeo stood to help her.

"No, please don't do that," Akari said, as was only polite, but Takeo gave her a small smile as he continued to clear the table.

"Your sister is kind and gracious," he said. "I must pay her back however I can."

"By being rude to her? Questioning her motives?" Akari shot back, not dropping his unkind hints at her character from earlier.

"Your sister has done a good thing," he said. "But it does not mean she could not have done a better one."

"If you are looking to confront fae prejudice in this town,"

Akari said, turning to Takeo and crossing her arms, "Yoshimi is not the person you need to be taking down. She does whatever she can for the fae in this region."

"Perhaps I should be confronting you instead?" he asked with a mischievous side smile.

"What is that supposed to mean?" Akari asked, her hackles up.

"You did not want to work with me," he said. "That was very clear."

"It isn't that I don't want to work with you," Akari said. "But given how anti-fae this town can be, I knew having a fae partner would be very difficult."

"Are you the sort of person to back down from a challenge?" Takeo asked, raising a brow. Turning, he put the last of the dishes away.

Akari's voice hitched in her throat. Of course she wasn't. So what was the real reason she didn't want to work with Takeo? She couldn't think of an answer that wouldn't confirm what he implied. She had never thought of herself as prejudiced, but she couldn't deny her distaste for working with Takeo other than because he was at least part fae.

He did not force her to reply, but he gave a small bow as he showed himself out.

"I will see you tomorrow, partner," he said as he shut the door.

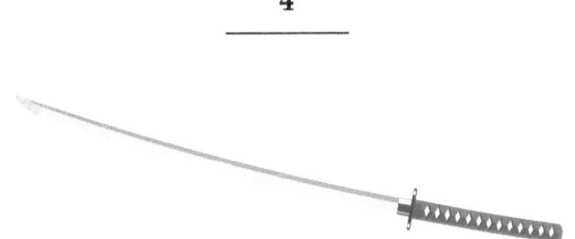

4

*T*he next morning, Akari left home early and went to Sera's dojo. Even though it was in Sera's home, the dojo was always open to any Sword Kissed who needed to practice. She wanted to find out more about Takeo before they really started working together. They were already clashing, and that was no way to work with someone, to be a partner. Who knew what they were facing, other than something dangerous. Her life might depend on her ability to trust Takeo. Right now, she wouldn't trust him to hold her katana.

As she snuck out of the house, she peeked in on Elwin. The boy was sleeping soundly, snuggled into his blanket on the futon. He looked safe, content. But she couldn't help but think about what Takeo had said. Maybe he would have felt even safer had he been placed with his own people. She'd never say it out loud, though. She wasn't ready to give Takeo the satisfaction. She slipped silently out of the house, locking the door behind her.

Cherry blossoms had wafted across the porch over her feet. She looked up, seeing the sakura tree in their yard was in full bloom. The bench under it looked decrepit, though. It had not been used for years, and it looked like it would crumble if anyone tried to sit on it. When she and Yoshimi had been little, their mother used to read to them on that bench. She hadn't sat there since her mother died.

Sera was not in the dojo yet when Akari arrived, which was what she was planning on. Sera had to have received some sort of information on Takeo, some background letter about who he was and his reputation in Ryu. Sera wouldn't have trusted him blindly. Akari snuck through the dojo and into Sera's office. There was a small desk low to the floor. Akari snuck over to it and opened the top drawer. The file would probably be easy enough to find since she would have just looked at it the day before. She was only mildly concerned about being caught rummaging through Sera's office. But if Sera found her, she already had her excuses planned out.

In the first drawer, she found nothing of importance, just blank paper, pens, and other odds and ends. In the top drawer on the left, she found a few reports relating to local crimes, but nothing she was working on. In the next drawer, though, she found several interesting files. She pulled out the missing person fliers. Takeo must have given them back to Sera for her to review. Akari flipped through them absently. Not really expecting to see anything new, her breath hitched when she saw Takeo looking at her from one of the pages.

She quickly realized it wasn't Takeo on the page, but someone who looked shockingly similar.

"Vesaris Torgwyn," she mumbled, reading the name. He looked older than Takeo, his face even more stern, but he had the same eyes and cheekbones. She wondered if the man was his elder brother, or possibly his father. Fae didn't tend to show their age the same way humans did, and their lifespans were twice as long.

The flier said Vesaris had vanished about six months ago from his home in Ryu. He had walked out his front door to check on his horses, but was never seen again. There was no sign of foul play and no reason to think he had abandoned his family, being known as a dedicated family member and upstanding member of the community.

Well, however this man was related to Takeo, it could certainly explain his interest in the case.

She put the flier back with the others before rummaging through the rest of the desk. She found more detailed case files about some of the missing people throughout the prefecture. These must have been files Sera had compiled. They were similar to the ones Takeo had brought. Underneath those, she found a folder with Takeo's name on it.

She opened it excitedly, curious about what she would find. There was a hand-drawn rendition of Takeo that was very well done. It did an excellent job of capturing his eyes and high cheekbones. She took it out of the folder, then smoothed it out on top of the missing person fliers.

Then she found some more general information about him. His father was fae, his mother human, as she suspected, and he was a fourth child. But there was no other information about his family, which she found annoying. She would have liked to have known more about where they were from and how his parents got together, but she supposed it wouldn't make much sense to include such personal information in the letter.

He had been working as an investigator for the human Ministry of Justice in Ryu for nearly ten years, starting as a desk clerk when he was only a teenager, but he quickly moved up the ranks due to his strong work ethic and because he had helped close several high-profile cases in his early days. He was an expert marksman, one of the best bowmen in all of Ryu. He came to Sera highly recommended.

That was it.

Akari sighed and closed the folder in annoyance. She hadn't learned much of anything about him.

"I appreciate your concerns..." she heard Sera say.

Akari quickly shoved Takeo's file back into the drawer, hurriedly slamming it as Sera and Takeo entered the room.

"Akari-chan," Sera gasped when she saw her standing by her desk. "What are you doing here?"

"Forgive me, Sensei," Akari said with a quick bow, grabbing the missing person fliers. "I wanted to get an early start and review the missing persons files again, hoping to find some sort of link or other information."

"I see..." Sera said, obviously annoyed. She made her way around the other side of her desk. Akari quickly moved toward the door and tried to shuffle past Takeo, but he stopped her.

"Did you find one?" Takeo asked.

"One what?" Akari asked, suddenly flustered.

"A link?" he clarified.

"Oh, not yet," she mumbled. "I need to look through these a bit more."

"You two better get started," Sera said. After opening her drawers, she picked through them. She was obviously concerned Akari had taken something else. Akari was irritated with herself for calling her honor into question to her sensei, but the mistake had been made.

"Yes, Sensei," Akari said. She rushed out of the building as quickly as she could, but she knew Takeo was right on her heels. She could hear his footsteps this time.

"Did you learn anything interesting about me?" Takeo asked as soon as they were outside.

Akari started for a moment, but then picked up her pace. "What are you talking about?" She hoped he was just guessing her real reason for being in Sera's office but didn't have any proof.

"That's what you were doing in there, right?" he asked, keeping in step with her stride. "You have the drawing of me from my folder on your stack of fliers there. Why else would you have it?"

Akari peered guiltily down at the fliers. She had forgotten she had laid his picture on top. She hoped Sera hadn't noticed, but of course Sera noticed everything.

Akari cleared her throat, winced, and held her head up. "If we are going to be working together, I think I need to know what I am getting into," she said.

"You could have just asked me," he said.

"Would you have answered all of my questions truthfully?" she asked.

He shrugged. "If I thought it was pertinent to the situation at hand."

"So, no," she said, feeling vindicated. "But I suppose you could ask Sera for information about my background if you want to be fair. I have nothing to hide."

"Actions will tell me more about you than a piece of paper," Takeo said.

Akari wasn't sure if this was meant to be an insult or not. What had he so far decided about her based on her actions? Probably nothing good. What exactly did Sera think Akari was going to get out of this partnership? Akari needed to turn this around. She needed to show him how capable she was. She thought about asking him about the flier for Vesaris, but she had the feeling he would be irritated by her prying. He would see she was more interested in finding out about his connection to the man than trying to find him. She studied the fliers one by one, pretending not to notice the similarities when she passed Vesaris's flier. She pulled out the flier of a young woman instead.

"Here, this woman," she said, handing a flier to Takeo. "She is from a village nearby. We should go there. Talk to the family. See if we can find out what happened to her."

Takeo nodded his agreement. "Lead the way," he said.

The village was not within walking distance, so they went to the stables to get some horses.

They rode out to a human village called Hashikami where

they were greeted by several welcoming people. None of them bothered to hide their stares at Takeo, but they were polite enough not to say anything and treated him cordially.

"We are looking for the family of Narita Toichi," Akari said.

"I am her okāsan," an older, frail woman said as she walked slowly toward Akari. "When I saw you coming, I had a feeling you were here about her."

Akari gave the older woman a deep, respectful bow. Takeo did the same. "I'm sorry for your loss," Akari said. "Will you tell me what happened?"

"What is to tell?" the woman asked. "One moment she was here, the next... *poof!*" She indicated the suddenness of Narita's disappearance with a popping movement of her hands.

Akari nodded. "Had anything strange happened before she vanished?" Akari pushed. "Did she have any enemies? An angry lover?" Akari's eyes scanned the crowd as she asked, hoping to see a reaction from someone. A mundane explanation for the woman's disappearance, while sad, would be preferable to some sort of magical cause.

"Not at all," the woman said. "Narita was a good girl. A basket weaver. No lovers."

Akari nodded, but it was odd for a young woman to have no possible suitors. There might have been someone in her life she hadn't told her mother about. "Had she mentioned seeing anything odd?" Akari asked. "Something she couldn't explain, or an encounter with a magical being or demon?"

"A demon?" the woman asked, then she shook her head. "I hope not. Nothing but problems!"

"What do you mean?" Akari asked.

The woman frowned, sticking out her lower lip. "We used to live in harmony with the creatures of the earth," she explained. "Some were tricksters. Yes, some were dangerous. But that is the way of life, and you learn to avoid them or placate them. Just like living near bears or a wild tiger."

Akari nodded. It was true most villages had their own way of dealing with the magical being said to inhabit the woods. It was rare a creature grew so aggressive a Sword Kissed had to be called in. But lately, their services were being called upon more and more often.

"But the creatures..." the old woman continued. "They have changed. So angry. So dark. For many years, we only tried to keep away from them and scare them away from the village. But recently, we have had to fight them off. And we warn the children not to ever approach them. Even if they want the creature to give them a good-luck charm. It is village policy to run away from and report any magical creatures."

"So you don't think she ran across one, maybe by accident?" Akari asked.

"She would have told me, I think," the woman said. "We try to warn each other if there is a creature nearby."

"Thank you," Akari said with a bow. "Do you mind if we explore the village and surrounding woods?"

"Please," the woman said. "Do whatever it takes to find my daughter."

Akari motioned for Takeo to follow her out of the village proper.

"What do you think?" she asked.

"Not much to go on," he said. "If there was no creature sighting, we have no idea what we are looking for."

Akari nodded. "It doesn't mean she didn't see one, though. She could have seen it right before her disappearance."

"Or it could have disguised itself as something safe," Takeo said. "If your zashiki-warashi could change into something frightening, it could also change into something normal. Something that would not cause alarm, like a cat or rabbit. Maybe even a tree!"

"Or she might not have seen it at all," Akari said. "Maybe it just saw her."

Akari surveyed their surroundings. They were in the woods now. This was an old forest. The trees were larger than she could reach around, and the foliage was so thick she could barely see the sky. They could hear the buzz of crickets and the caw of birds in their nests.

When she turned toward Takeo, she saw he was standing with his eyes closed and his hands palm-up.

"What are you doing?" she asked.

"Listening," he said. "Feeling..."

Akari figured this must be a fae thing. She knew fae had a connection to the magical energies of the earth, which was why many humans did not trust them. Some humans considered fae to be more akin to demons than humans. Akari believed all magic in the world was connected, but she did not think all magic was inherently evil. She couldn't. How else could she explain or accept her own Sword Kissed abilities?

"Do you sense anything?" Akari asked.

"There is something..." he said, his face twitching. "But it is faint. I cannot tell if it is weak, or simply old. Something fading with time...Wait..."

He gasped, suddenly flung to the ground by an unseen force. Akari drew her sword and ran to his side.

"What is it?" she yelled. She swung her gaze left and right but saw nothing. "Where did it go?"

His breath had been knocked out, and he struggled to breathe in. "I...I don't know," he gasped.

Akari stood. She ran back to where Takeo had been standing before he was knocked down. "Where are you?" she yelled.

She heard a low rumbling laugh. It sounded like the same voice the zashiki-warashi had after it had transformed into a beast. The sound was coming from deeper into the forest. She bolted after it.

"Akari," Takeo yelled after her, but she did not wait for him. What could he do anyway? He wasn't Sword Kissed. He didn't have a light he could transfer into a weapon to fight the darkness of demons.

Only she could stop this creature—whatever it was.

Akari stopped and listened. The forest was nearly silent, but Akari was not afraid.

"I know you are here," she said.

"And I know you," a feminine voice said. Akari moved her head slowly around, but she saw nothing. It was the same voice she heard before. She was sure of it. What was the woman doing here? How did she know Akari would come? It was by pure accident she chose Narita's flier to follow up on. No one could have known ahead of time she was coming. Whoever this woman was, she was more than any mere demon. She had superior powers. Powers that Akari should be leery of. But Akari couldn't back down now. She had to attack while she had the chance. She had to find her.

"Show yourself," Akari said, holding her sword up by her head. "I am Sword Kissed Tanaka, and I will cut you down."

"Then why would I show myself?" the woman asked.

"You are a coward," Akari said. "You attack defenseless villagers, children. But you would not dare attack a woman of strength."

Akari felt a hard blow to her back, which knocked her to the ground. She landed on her knees and palms, hard. She winced in pain, but she was not out. She still held a firm grip on her sword. After she jumped to her feet, she swung her sword behind her as the turned in the direction the blow had come from, but there was nothing there. She held her sword up.

"Another cowardly move," Akari said. "Attacking me from behind. Where is your honor, beast?"

"I know more of honor than you could imagine," the voice said, floating around her. Akari tried to follow the sound, but it was both everywhere and nowhere. "I sacrificed everything..."

The voice growled and hissed, as if it was struggling with something.

"What did you sacrifice?" Akari asked. "Who are you?"

"Sakura...sakura..." the voice said. "The end is not yet. There is time..." The voice let out a scream.

"Time for what?" Akari asked, turning around frantically. "Who is sakura? Why are you saying that?"

Akari felt a punch to her gut, then to her chin, and she staggered backward. Something large and dark appeared before her.

"It is too late, Sword Kissed," the darkness rumbled. "The world is at an end."

Akari tried to stand, but the pain in her abdomen was sharp.

"Whoever you are," Akari said. "I will stop you."

The creature laughed. "You? You are nothing."

An arrow flew through the creature, and it yelped in pain. Takeo ran forward, and then sliced at the darkness with his daggers.

The creature growled at Takeo and took a swipe at him with its claws, but he weaved out of the way. The creature snarled in frustration before dissolving into the air and blowing away.

"Come back, you bastard," Takeo yelled into the wind.

"What the hell was that?" Akari and Takeo asked at the same time. Akari used her sword to help her get to her feet.

"Damn it, Akari!" Takeo snapped. In angry motions, he collected his arrows that had fallen to the ground or gotten stuck in trees. "Why didn't you wait for me?"

Akari sheathed her sword. "What the hell were you doing attacking the beast? It was talking. I could have learned something useful!"

"You were flat on your back," Takeo said. "The beast had the advantage. I was helping you..."

"I don't need your help," Akari said. "I can defend myself."

"We are a team, Akari," Takeo said. "You should have waited for me. We could have taken the demon down right now before it had a chance to kill anyone else, but you let it get away!"

"I'm Sword Kissed," Akari said in a huff. "You are not. I don't need your help. You are just slowing me down."

Takeo chuckled and rolled his eyes. He sheathed his daggers and gave Akari a curt bow. "Whatever you say, *Sword Kissed*. What do you think we should do now, Miss High-and-Mighty?"

Akari rolled her eyes and pressed her lips. What was he doing now? Sera would somehow hear of this, and she would have an earful for Akari about it; she was sure of that. But Takeo would take none of the blame, even though he had been less than useless to her. Yeah, he had sent that demon packing, but only for now. He didn't defeat it. It wasn't possible. The demon was only biding its time.

"We should head back to the village," Akari said with a huff. "Let them know the forest is not safe."

Takeo agreed, but they walked slowly and surely back in case the mysterious entity reappeared.

When they arrived back at the village, Akari went to visit with Narita's mother while Takeo told the rest of the villagers to avoid the woods at all costs. She pulled out the other missing person fliers, but she was sure to grab Takeo's picture out of the stack and shove it into her pocket.

"Do any of these people look familiar?" Akari asked her. "I am wondering if there is any connection between them."

Narita's mother looked at each picture carefully, but she shook her head over each one. "I do not know any of these people. Oh, this one..." She stopped at the flier for Vesaris. "This man... Is that...?" She nodded toward Takeo with a little hopefulness in her voice.

"Oh, no," Akari said. "I'm sorry, but it's not him. It is one of his kin."

The woman nodded sadly. She probably hoped Takeo had been missing at one point but had been found safe. Akari felt guilty for getting the woman's hopes up like that. She reminded herself she should probably remove Vesaris's flier from the stack as well to avoid any confusion in the future.

When the woman came to Narita's picture, her breath hitched and she put her hand to her mouth. "My beautiful girl," she said shakily.

"We won't give up," Akari said. "We will keep looking for her, for all of them."

"There is something wrong," the old woman said. She pulled a pencil out of her pocket. "Who did this drawing? He should be punished." She drew something on the picture before handing it back to Akari. She had drawn a large wine-stain birthmark over the girl's left eye and cheek.

Akari gave the mother a kindly smile. "The mark made your daughter unique." It could also explain why the woman had no lovers. For many old-fashioned people, they would consider a distinct facial mark to be an ill omen.

The old woman nodded. "She was never ashamed of it. Proud even! She could not hide her strength. It was plain for all to see."

Akari nodded and hoped she would have a chance to meet this brave woman, but she doubted it.

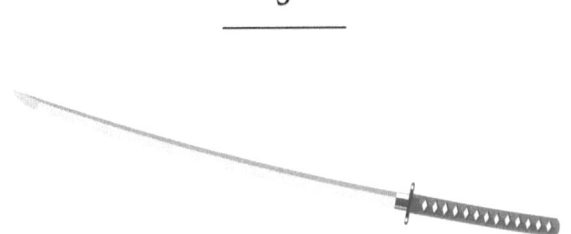

5

*A*kari could not help but feel defeated as they made their way back to town. She was no closer to finding an answer or to stopping whatever was causing the disappearances. But she couldn't let her "partner" know how she felt. It was clear Takeo blamed her for the demon getting away, which galled her. What right did he have to criticize her? She had been training for over a decade to take down demons. What did he know about it? Fae might have some useful skills beyond humans, but nothing like she had. This was her job, her so-called calling. She had been born for it. No one could be harder or more disappointed in her than she could.

Except possibly Sera. She did not look forward to facing her sensei when they returned.

"You have not lost yet," Takeo said, seemingly able to read her thoughts. His voice sounded tight, as if it was taking a great effort for him to speak to her. "Do not carry defeat like a stone. We have enough to carry already."

Surprised, she peered at him, and he gave her a slight hint of a smile. She assumed he was trying to be encouraging, so she gave him a nod. She still didn't fully trust him, or think his presence was particularly useful, but he was here. There was nothing either of them could do about that.

"We will get another chance," she said. "The creature will strike again."

"So we wait for it to kill someone else?" he asked. They eyed each other, and Akari wondered which one of them looked angrier.

"We don't know what we are facing," she finally said. "Zashiki-warashi. Shadows. Invisible monsters. Whatever this thing is, it could strike anywhere, anytime. In any form! There's no pattern to the attacks. How am I supposed to predict what its next move will be?"

"Enough people have already died," he spat. "We have to do more."

The image of Vesaris Torgwyn crinkled in Akari's pocket.

"Is there something you need to tell me?" she asked.

"What are you talking about?" he asked, exasperated.

"Something about this case...these cases that you aren't telling me?" she asked, raising an eyebrow. "What really made you investigate them?"

A flicker crossed his face before he turned to stare down the road that seemed to stretch endlessly before them. He was quiet for so long, Akari thought he wasn't going to reply.

"It doesn't matter," he finally said. "Someone needed to find the answer. Someone had to give a damn. And if it isn't going to be the Sword Kissed, why not me?"

"What makes you think I don't give a damn?" Akari asked, her own annoyance revving up. "I'm doing my best here."

"Are you?" he asked. "I can see in your eyes you don't really care about any of these people. This is just a job to you."

"Okay, you are way out of line here—" she started to say, but he cut her off.

"I think I'm right inside the lines," he said. "And I can see what's going on here way more clearly than you."

"Oh, really?" she asked. "You sure lost your temper back there. And I know you have a more personal connection to these cases than you are letting on, so don't talk to me about seeing clearly."

"What the hell are you talking about?" he asked. Frustrated eyes swung to her. He twisted in his saddle to face her full on.

"You know damn well—"

They heard a scream. A woman ran toward them, wild with fright. They jumped off their horses. Takeo took the woman in his arms while Akari drew her sword.

"Help me," the woman screamed. "It was right behind me!"

"What?" Akari asked. As she looked down the road, she saw nothing but a couple of leaves blowing in the wind.

"The blackness," the woman said, sobbing into Takeo's shirt. "I...I can't explain except it was dark. Just darkness."

Akari's eyes shot to Takeo. She wasn't sure why she didn't remember what little Elwin had said at dinner the night before.

Shadow, she mouthed. A light went off behind his eyes, and he nodded.

"You could say that what I felt knock me down was a shadow," he said softly.

"Where are you from?" Akari asked the girl.

"Yahakami, near the sea," the girl said.

"Elwin's parents, the entity in the forest, Yahakami village," Akari said. "All shadows."

"And you said blackness seeped out of the zashiki-warashi," Takeo added. "It's certainly related."

"Please," the girl begged. "My village is under attack. The shadow, she has been seen before. I escaped, but it followed me. But you must go there, Sword Kissed! You must help my people!"

"Head to Nasu city," Takeo told the girl as he held her face comfortingly. "You will be safe there."

She stared up at him affectionately, then her eyes fell on his ears and she took a step back. She looked at Akari with confusion on her face. Akari said nothing, and the girl eventually continued running toward Nasu. Takeo paused for a moment as he watched her run away. As usual, Akari could not read the expression on his face. Was he hurt? Angry? She wasn't sure and decided not to try to guess. She got back on her horse.

"If we ride hard, we can be in Yahakami village in a couple of hours," she said.

"Will we be there before sundown?" he asked. "It would be impossible to try to trap a shadow at night."

Akari peered up at the sun and saw it was still before noon. "I think so," she said. "But we won't have long. We will have to work fast."

He nodded, and they both urged their horses to run.

$\mathcal{W}$hen they finally approached the village of Yahakami, Akari and Takeo, and their horses, were exhausted, but they still had a couple hours of daylight left. As they made their way down the main road, they were surprised there were no people outside.

"It's like a ghost town," Akari said gloomily.

Takeo nodded and tied his horse to the nearest hitching post. "Is anyone here?" he called.

Akari looked from building to building, finally noticing a few faces peeking out some windows.

"We are here to help," she said, drawing her katana. "I am

Sword Kissed Tanaka, and this is my partner, Takeo Torgwyn. You do not need to fear us."

She heard the squeak of a door behind her. Turning, she saw a middle-aged man step out onto his porch.

"There is an evil here," he said.

Akari nodded. "We heard about the shadow demon," she said. "We have been trying to track it."

"It is an enenra," the man said. "A woman of smoke."

"Of course," Akari said, turning to Takeo. "An enenra, a smoke demon. That could be mistaken for a shadow."

Takeo nodded. "Where was the enenra last seen?"

The man's eyes welled up with tears, but he did his best to control his emotions. "It...it took my wife," he said. He pointed west. "Toward the old ruins. I tried to grab her, to bring her back. To save her. But the monster...as soon as it touched my wife, Itami, it looked like she became an enenra, too! I couldn't touch her. My hands went right through her like an illusion!"

Akari shot Takeo a glance, and their faces must have mirrored their concern. Akari had never heard of a demon turning a person into one of their kind before. This was a terrifying development.

"Stay in your homes," Takeo said, and the man retreated inside, closing the door behind him. Then Takeo and Akari headed in the direction the man had pointed.

"A demon able to turn people into demons," Takeo mumbled. "Do you know what this means?"

"The demons could be multiplying," she said. "We need to stop this one before it takes anyone else."

"Have you fought an enenra before?" Takeo asked.

"No," Akari admitted. "But my sensei has taught me how."

Takeo nodded and look up at the sky. "The evening is coming quickly. Too quickly."

Akari looked up and noticed a few twilight stars could

already be seen, but by her calculations, it should only be late afternoon.

"This whole place is cursed," she said through gritted teeth.

Just then, they heard a scream.

They ran toward the ruins—large metal structures leftover from the days when the world was still in one piece. The dimming sky created long shadows over the place. Akari looked around, but she did not see anything unusual at first.

"Where are you?" she called out.

"Help me," someone screamed. She and Takeo ran toward the sounds.

They finally glimpsed a woman being dragged by her hair behind one of the structures by a dark creature.

"There," Akari yelled. Takeo nocked an arrow and then let it fly, but it flew right through the creature like nothing was there. "Come on!"

Akari and Takeo ran toward the woman, but when they got around the corner, all they saw was the smoky shape of a woman. The corporeal form she had been dragging was gone.

Akari held her sword up. "Where is the woman you stole?" Akari asked.

"Sakura...sakura..." the shadow said.

"Who are you? What do you want?" Akari demanded

The creature laughed. "Are you a fairy, sakura of mine..."

"*Stop* singing that song," Akari yelled. Out of the corner of her eye, she saw Takeo shoot her a look, but she didn't take her eyes off the monster. "Tell me who you are!"

"She is coming...sakura...sakura..." the creature said as she started to drift away on a breeze.

"No, you *don't*," Akari yelled. She sliced her katana across her hand, cutting her hand open and getting her blood on the blade. She gasped in pain, but her katana began to glow with a blue aura. She could feel the flesh of her hand stitching itself back together as she ran toward the enenra and swung her sword.

The demon seemed to have been caught off guard. It tried to float away more quickly, but it could not. It drifted left and right, but Akari was able to predict its movements. She cut the demon quickly across the chest, then the abdomen. The creature screamed in pain.

"Sakura! Sakura," it yelled, but the smoke seemed to solidify. It turned thick and black like tar before melting to the ground.

Akari looked around, but there was still no sign of the woman the enenra had been dragging. "Where did she go?" Akari asked.

"I don't know," Takeo said. "She seems to have...vanished..."

"Shit," Akari said. "But what made her vanish? Was it the enenra? Or a zashiki-warashi? Or...or still something else? Why does it seem like every step closer we get only leads us down another winding path?"

Takeo shook his head. "I don't know. But we should keep looking around here. Maybe we can still find her."

Akari looked up at the sky. "The light is nearly gone."

"Then we better search quickly," Takeo said with a nod. "We need to leave this place by dark."

"We should split up then," Akari said. "Cover more ground."

Takeo hesitated, but then nodded and headed down a row between the metal structures while Akari went straight.

She walked quietly, but quickly. They needed to cover as much ground as possible before it was too late. Akari rounded a corner, catching sight of a small smoke creature darting away from her.

"I see one," she called to Takeo.

The creature was fast, too fast! It was getting away from her. Suddenly, Takeo appeared at the end of the row. Akari spent half a second considering how he could have gotten there so quickly, but when the creature saw Takeo, it quickly turned back to her, as if it forgot she was there. It shrank back when it saw her, but it was too late. By the time it turned back to face Takeo, Akari was right behind it. She quickly ran it through with her still-glowing sword, and it melted to the ground in a puddle of tar.

"Where there are two..." Akari panted.

"There are going to be more," Takeo completed for her. She nodded. "Still no sign of the missing wife."

"Let's keep going," Akari said. "If we can kill more creatures, we might have a chance of finding her."

Takeo nodded, and then headed down another side path. Akari turned in the opposite direction. She moved stealthily, but then felt a chill down her back. She glanced up to see the sun had nearly set. They were almost out of time.

"Itami," Akari called for the missing wife. "We are here! Where are you?" She listened and heard a strangled scream. She ran toward it, but still could not see anything. "I'm here," she yelled, but there was no reply.

Takeo ran up to her. "What are you doing?" he asked in an angered whisper. "The enenra will find us."

"All the better," Akari said in a normal voice. "We are out of time!"

Takeo held up his hand to quiet her. He was looking down at their feet. When Akari dipped her head as well, she saw what he was staring at. Smoke was seeping out of the metal structure they were standing next to and entwining around their ankles. Takeo reached down, and then gripped the handle to lift the door. Akari nodded, and he thrust the door up.

Akari's glowing sword lit up the inside of the structure. In the middle of the room collapsed to the ground were two women.

And they were surrounded by a dozen enenra.

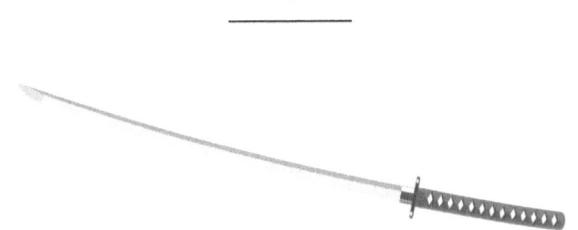

6

The smoke demons raised hazy heads at Akari and Takeo, and then opened their mouths in silent screams. Akari stepped back. One demon at a time, she could handle. But so many all at once? She hesitated and shot a look at Takeo. While she could technically light any weapon with her blood, it would fade and return to normal as soon as he took it back. He could not fight with a Sword Kissed weapon against a demon.

Akari tightened her grip on her katana and prepared to advance. If she went down, at least she would take a few of the monsters with her. As darkness fell, the smoke demons became harder to see. If Akari was going to fight them, it would have to be now. She took a deep breath and opened her mouth to let out a yell, but she then heard several battle cries come from behind her.

She swung around to see several of her fellow Sword Kissed running toward the metal structure, their illuminated katanas held aloft. As they charged the demons, Akari joined them. The creatures knew they had lost and tried to escape the structure, but the Sword Kissed blocked the exit, and the rest of the structure was air tight. Even their formless bodies of smoke could not escape. As the Sword Kissed swung their weapons through the hazy forms, the smoke eventually cleared, and all that stood in the structure were the people with physical forms.

"Are you all right, Akari-chan?" her friend Kaya asked her as she sheathed her sword.

"I'm better now that you are here," Akari said, gripping her arm. "What are you doing here?"

"The woman you met on the road," Kaya explained. "She made her way into town and told us what happened. When Sera-sensei heard you were heading out to the village on your own, she thought you would need the support of your sisters. The village chief told us you had come out here."

Akari nodded. "It is good you came. The past encounters had only been with one creature at a time. I did not expect there to be so many here."

Kaya laughed and slapped her arm. "That is what you get for leaving me out."

"Believe me," Akari whispered. "I wish Sera had made you my partner instead."

"Akari-san!" Takeo called from across the room, and Akari blushed. She hoped he hadn't heard her. Twisting toward him, she saw he was crouched over the bodies the enenra had been hovering around.

She walked over to him. One body was of a middle-aged woman. The other was of a younger woman, but on her face was the distinct port-wine stain the old mother from Hashikami village had drawn on her daughter's picture. Takeo shook his head.

The girl's eyes were open, but they were black, empty, soulless. Her life force had been completely drained. Takeo reached out and closed her eyelids. He then placed his hand to his mouth to hide his emotions. She had the feeling he had seen this before.

Kaya came over and stood behind Akari. She gasped. "What the hell happened?" she asked. "Enenra do not do this."

Akari nodded. "Enenra simply choke their victims, like normal smoke. This is not an enenra attack. And where is the wife they stole from Yahakami village?"

"So what are we really dealing with?" Takeo asked as he stood. "What is using magical beasts to steal humans and fae and then draining them of their life force?"

Akari shook her head. She had no idea, and she was not looking forward to finding out.

hat night, the villagers asked the Sword Kissed and Takeo to stay as their honored guests. It was too late for them to travel back to the city, and the villagers were still afraid of the enenra. Akari wanted to stay as well and see if she could learn more about whatever they were supposed to be hunting.

The man whose wife had gone missing was the village chief, and his name was Ichiro. He hosted a large dinner in the communal hall and sat next to Akari, but he was obviously still distraught and did not speak much. The entire gathering was subdued. It was hardly a night for celebrating. The chief's wife had been killed, along with the girl from the other village. Elwin's parents were also dead. Akari suspected that anyone who had gone missing was probably dead.

But they weren't just killing or transforming people into demons. They were draining their life force. But why? And who would have the power to do this? Akari shook her head. She had no idea. She decided to try and talk to the chief, either to get more answers or to distract herself from the gravity of the situation.

"Tell me more about your wife, Chief Ichiro," Akari said. She bit into a delicious freshly caught fish.

The side of Chief Ichiro's mouth twitched up. "We grew up together," he said. "We have spent nearly every day of our lives together. We went to school together, then married young. We have three small children of our own."

Akari nodded, dipping her head to survey her food. It suddenly tasted like ash in her mouth. Everyone they knew of who had gone missing were well-loved in their communities. She tried to remain distant from her work. Emotional attachment made the job too hard. This was one of those times she wished she had not asked for more information.

From across the room, she heard a laugh. She saw Endo smiling and enjoying the company of two young men. Akari shook her head in disgust. How could Endo be so rude as to flirt after what they had just seen? But at the same time, she envied her. Wasn't that why she had spoken to Chief Ichiro right now? As a distraction? Akari was cold, but Endo was an iceberg. Nothing fazed her. Right now, Akari wished she could stop caring enough to focus on what she needed to do next, but her mind was whirling. She needed to get out of there.

Akari pushed away from the table and stood. She gave Chief Ichiro a bow. "I will go patrol the edges of the village. Thank you for your hospitality."

He gave her a nod back. From across the room, she caught sight of Takeo watching her. She quickly averted her eyes and headed out of the hall.

She stood in the light of the bonfires that had been lit around the village. The people were—understandably—afraid of the dark, so they had done their best to create as much artificial light to get through the night as possible. Akari watched the shadows the flames created dance and sway across the ground and buildings. She was trying to see if any dark movements were unnatural, something she should be on guard against, but the more she stared, the more blurred her vision became. The dancing shadows threatened to lull her to sleep even as she was standing. She shook her head and walked through some of the village dwellings, away from the fires and toward the beach.

The moon was bright and full, and it shone down on the waves that gently lapped the shore. She took in a deep, cleansing breath and slowly exhaled.

"It is not safe..." a voice said. She drew her sword and spun around, bringing the blade down and stopping it right at the tip of Takeo's nose. "To be out here alone," he continued, his eyes glued to the blade, but he did not even flinch.

She pulled her sword back and sheathed it. "It is not safe to try to sneak up on a Sword Kissed either," she said as she turned back to the sea.

He took another step and stood next to her. "What exactly is a Sword Kissed?" he asked.

"As darkness filled the world, the light of one woman shone —" she started to recite, but he interrupted her.

"I know that," he said with a chuckle. "I have heard the stories, the legends, the same as anyone. But I have never met a Sword Kissed until now. How would *you* describe what you are?"

Akari licked the salty sea spray from her lips before she spoke. It was always difficult to try to explain what being Sword Kissed meant to her.

"It is like being full of light in a dark place," she finally said. "As if I could hold the whole world in my arms and make everything better...yet knowing you can't."

Takeo gave a slow nod.

"It is hope and fear, happiness and sadness, love and betrayal rolling inside of me all at the same time," she continued. "It is as if I am always at war with myself because something—some integral part—is missing that would bring peace and balance."

"So it is not the presence of something special, but the lack of it?" Takeo asked.

"In a way," Akari said as she rubbed her arms, suddenly feeling chilled. "No one knows the true origins of the Sword Kissed. Have we always been? Were we created for a singular purpose? Did we just...appear out of the ashes of the Great Divide? Are we human? Are we fae? Are we...something else?" She shook her head. "There are only questions, and so few answers."

"You think the Sword Kissed could be fae?" he asked. "I have never heard that before."

"My parents were human," Akari said. "I know they were. And Yoshimi is human. Every Sword Kissed has human parents. We are human, but we are also something more. But if we dwell on what that something is, it could lead to...problems."

Takeo nodded. "You mean you don't want to risk humans casting you out and treating you as badly as they treat fae."

Akari gave a sad nod. "Something like that."

"What about you then?" he asked. "If you have a bit of an inkling about what it means to be discriminated against, why do you not do more to help the fae?"

Akari felt the hairs on the back of her neck bristle, but she tried to calm them down. It was a fair question, and one she had wrestled with herself, but one so complicated she preferred to not try to answer it.

"I do what I can for all people," she said. "I protect humans and fae from the monsters in the world. When I look at Yoshimi, I know I could do more. I admit that. I..." She sighed. "Anything I say to try to justify myself will only sound like an excuse. So I'll not insult you by saying anything."

Takeo gave her a smile. "Thank you for your honesty," he said.

Akari smiled back. "Will you be honest with me?" she asked. He nodded. "You are half fae and half human. What must that be like? Are there more families in Ryu like yours?"

He chuckled. "There are a few," he said. "But it is not easy. There are many people who think we are unnatural. No better than the demons who seem to grow stronger every day."

He bent down and picked up a seashell, running his fingers over it to knock the sand loose.

"I know the hate and fear that exists between humans and fae all too well," he said. "But I also know love can exist and overcome all that. My parents loved each other very much."

"Loved?" Akari asked, but the word nearly caught in her throat.

He gave a small, single nod, but he did not continue.

Akari turned back to the sea, deciding not to ask for more information. She could see there was pain in his face behind his words. For the first time, she could see through his carefully crafted mask. She reached into her pocket, and then pulled out the flier for Vesaris Torgwyn. She handed it to him.

Taking the flier, he examined it affectionately. He ran his fingers over the soft parchment.

"I didn't say goodbye," he finally said. "I was helping Mother with the dishes. He said he was going to check the horses. I think I grunted or said okay or something stupid and then went back to stacking plates. And that was it."

He paused for a long time, and Akari didn't push him to continue. She just waited.

"It wasn't until after I had already gone to bed when Mother knocked on my door and asked me to go check on him," he said. "He had never come back in. I didn't even notice! What kind of son is that?"

"You didn't know," Akari said. "You couldn't have."

"But I should have been more attentive," he said. "I should

have been a better son. I should have said goodbye. Should have noticed when he didn't come back."

Akari wanted to try to comfort him, but she knew nothing she could say would help. He blamed himself, and it didn't matter how reasonable it was he shouldn't, his grief was something he was going to have to work through on his own.

"The last thing I said to my mother was 'don't forget to sew my skirt," Akari said. A weird chuckle escaped her throat. "What a stupid thing to say. By the time I got to the hospital, she was already gone. When I got home two days later, the skirt was lying on my bed—the hem perfectly repaired. I never wore the damn thing again."

"I'm beginning to see why Sera-sensei put us together," Takeo said with an ironic laugh. "We are quite a pair."

"Did you..." Akari paused. "Sorry, this is really insensitive. But did your father...was he like the women we found today?"

Takeo nodded. "It's not insensitive. It's pertinent to the case. And yes, he was like them."

"So what does it all mean?" Akari said with a sigh. "The demon isn't just killing, but it is draining the life force from humans and fae. Why?"

"When we catch it," Takeo said. "We can ask it."

Akari let out a small laugh, probably the only genuine one she had let escape her chest in weeks. She had to respect his optimism.

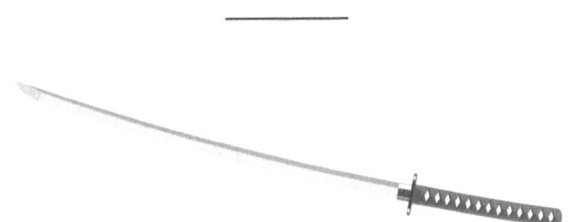

7

*T*he next day, Akari, Takeo, and the rest of the Sword Kissed spent most the sunlight hours patrolling the woods, the beach, and the ruins around Yahakami village. They found no other signs of any enenra or any other rogue demons. With a solemn nod, Chief Ichiro acknowledged they had done all they could for the village for now.

"If we learn anything new," Akari said with a bow, "we will return."

"May the Light bless you," Chief Ichiro said with a bow. All the other villagers had also gathered around them, and they all bowed in unison as the group mounted their horses and rode out of town.

Kaya trotted up next to Akari. "So, what is the next move?" she asked.

"I am not certain," Akari said. "We stopped the enenra for now, but we didn't learn anything new. We just have more questions. I'm not sure where to look next or how to protect people from another demon attack. So far, the attacks seem random. I feel like all I can do is wait for the next tragedy."

Kaya nodded and clicked her tongue at her horse to keep it walking straight. "What do you think, though?" she asked. "Did you see that woman's eyes? I felt like...like I was falling into them. I can still feel it." She shuddered.

"Yeah," Akari reluctantly agreed. "I do."

"What do you think it means?" Kaya asked.

"I don't know," Akari said. "Can you think of any creature, any legends, that talk about sucking someone's life force out of them?"

Kaya shook her head. "Not that I know of, but I can head to the archives when we get back. Maybe something there will jog my memory."

Akari doubted that. The "archives" were not particularly well-stocked or useful. So much of the world had been destroyed during the Great Divide: homes, schools, libraries, databases. Much knowledge from before was simply lost as well. The archives only contained information that had been collected since the Great Divide. Initially, people had rushed to write down anything they could remember from before—*The Tale of the Genji*, *The Revenge of the Forty-Seven Ronin*, and the poems of Fukuda Chiyo-ni were popular even now. But everyone knew that most of the world's knowledge had simply been forgotten.

"I have a feeling that what we are dealing with is older than anything in the archives," Akari said.

Kaya kicked her horse into a trot. "But we don't have anything older than the archives. If the answer isn't there, where are we supposed to find it?"

Akari urged her horse to keep up with Kaya's. "Maybe Sera knows something. She...always seems to know things the rest of us don't."

Kaya nodded. It was something everyone knew, yet no one talked about. Sera was a fixture in town, someone everyone knew and respected. Her knowledge and wisdom were unquestioned. But how she came to be who she was? That was something that no one could answer. Akari wasn't sure she even wanted to know the answer. Part of Sera's strength was in her mystique. To shatter that, to bring Sera down to the level of everyone else, wouldn't help anyone. Who wanted just some random lady to be training the Sword Kissed—the women who were supposed to be protecting everyone from the dark evils of the world?

"I'm still going to head to the archives," Kaya said. "Good luck with Sera."

*W*hen they arrived back in town, Akari went to see Sera, and Takeo followed her.

"What happened out there?" Sera asked with little welcome.

Akari gave a quick explanation of the enenra and how they had been vanquished. She also told Sera about the drained body of the missing women from the villages.

Sera crossed her arms and stood at a window. "What do you think we are dealing with?" she asked.

"I have no idea," Akari said. "Kaya is going to the archives to try and find information, but I think that what we are dealing with is very, very old in order to be so powerful."

Sera looked at Takeo. "And you? What do you think?"

"Akari is right that this thing, whatever it is, is powerful. Kaya is smart to look for more answers, but...I fear the answer has been lost to time."

Sera turned to Akari. "So what is your next step?"

Akari shrugged. "I'm not sure. I feel like all I can do is wait for the next killing."

Takeo tilted his head, pressing his lips with a shake of his head. He might not like it, but he had no idea of what to do next either, Akari knew.

"That's unacceptable," Sera said. "How many people are going to have to die before you are able to make progress?"

The words felt like a sword to the stomach. She was doing her best, working as quickly as possible. Did she not just take down a whole warehouse full of enenra? What more did Sera want from her?

"I'm sorry, Sensei," Akari said with a bow. "What would you like me to do?"

"Have you spoken to your partner at all about this?" Sera asked.

Akari shot a glance to Takeo, who was standing stoically. "We...have been speaking and working together..." she started to say.

"Have you?" Sera asked. "Because I'm not seeing much team work here. You've mentioned working with and talking to Kaya, and while Kaya is a competent Sword Kissed, *she* isn't your partner. Takeo is."

"Yes, Sensei," Akari said with another bow. "I will do better, Sensei."

Sera shook her head. "While you are waiting for the next death, I'm sending you on a training exercise. One designed to build teamwork."

Akari scoffed. "I know I have failed you, Sensei," she said. "But this hardly seems necessary. And such a waste of time—"

"You dare to question my methods?" Sera asked. Akari stopped talking. She wasn't in a position to argue. She would have to do whatever Sera ordered her to do.

"No, Sensei," Akari said through gritted teeth.

"Good," Sera said, opening a drawer and pulling out a map. "Pack an overnight bag. This is where you are going. Bring me a nightbloom from the caves under the ruins. I expect you back in two days."

Akari took the map from Sera and then bowed her way out of the room. "Yes, Sensei," she said. Takeo bowed out of the room as well.

Akari looked at the map. It was strange. She wasn't aware of any ruins on the mountain that loomed over Nasu, but she had never been there before.

"I must apologize," Takeo said. "I have not been a good partner."

Akari waved him off. "No, I was the one who ran off without you. Don't worry about it. Besides, Sera has always been harder on me than anyone else. I'm a constant disappointment."

"Why do you think that is?" he asked. "About her being harder on you," he clarified. "Not about you being a disappointment."

"I'm not sure," she said, stuffing the map into her pocket. "Well, I'm the only Sword Kissed she trained personally. She probably just has higher standards for me."

Takeo nodded. "I know what it is like to have an exacting mentor."

"I assume you succeeded at everything you ever attempted," Akari said in an attempt at levity, but it obviously had fallen flat when she saw Takeo's unsmiling face.

"I do not know why you would assume that," he said. "We all fail sometimes. But failure can also make us stronger."

"Take it easy," Akari said. "I only meant..." She sighed. Maybe the fae didn't have the same sense of humor humans did. "Never mind. I am going to go home and pack. Let's meet by the east gate in an hour."

Takeo gave her a small bow and walked away. She watched him for a moment, and she noticed several other women in the area observing him as well. They blushed and quickly turned away when they saw her looking at them. Akari had to admit that by any standard, Takeo was attractive. But she didn't imagine anything coming from it. They were making strides to work together, but nothing more. Besides, she couldn't imagine trying to have a relationship with a fae. It would be too difficult, too much too overcome. Just look at Yoshimi. No other human would be better suited to marry a fae than her and even she had not attempted it. What chance would someone like Akari have? She shook her head and turned for home.

It was nearly noon, so Yoshimi was there with Elwin, fixing a quick lunch of rice and steamed vegetables.

"I didn't expect you to be here," Yoshimi said. "I'm afraid I didn't fix enough. But there are some onigiri you can eat."

Akari placed some onigiri in a cloth and tied them up. Then she put them into a bag. "Yeah," she said. "These will be good for the road anyway."

"The road?" Yoshimi asked. She fixed a bowl of food for Elwin and herself. "Are you going somewhere?"

"Sera is sending Takeo and me on a training mission," she said, pulling the map from her pocket and handing it to Yoshimi. "Have you ever been out here before?"

Yoshimi took the map and studied it, her brow scrunching in confusion. "What did she say was out there? I didn't know there was anything out that way except for trees and rocks."

"I thought the same thing," Akari said, grabbing a few kinds of tsukemono and putting them in a small metal container and some fruit and putting all of it into her food bag. "But she says there are ruins at the top, and caves underneath where night-bloom grow."

"Nightbloom?" Yoshimi asked incredulously, handing the map back to Akari. She started to say something else, but then bit her tongue.

"What?" Akari asked.

Yoshimi shook her head and picked at her food. "It's a training mission, so I shouldn't say anything. I'm sure Sera has her reasons for sending you out there."

"Where the nightbloom grow
Is where my heart will find you
She waits there also."

Elwin uttered the haiku between bites of daikon.

Akari and Yoshimi both looked at him.

"What was that?" Yoshimi asked.

"Nothing," he said. "A poem about nightbloom."

"I've never heard it before," Akari said.

He shrugged. "A fae poem."

Akari couldn't suppress a smile at the edge of her mouth. She noticed Yoshimi was smiling, too. For a little man of few words, he sure knew how to throw Akari some serious shade.

"Who is she?" Akari asked when she had collected herself.

Elwin shrugged again and looked at Yoshimi. "Can I have a mochi? I finished my rice."

"Of course, dear," Yoshimi said, and Elwin happily ran over to the counter to pick out a mochi generously rolled in powdered sugar.

"Do you know what he's talking about?" Akari asked.

Yoshimi shook her head. "The fae, like us, have many legends and stories about things, including nightbloom. Of course, a flower that blooms and glows in the dark is going to be credited with having supernatural abilities or meaning."

"I'll be sure to bring one back for you," Akari said as she finished packing her bag.

"It's just..." Yoshimi paused.

"What?" Akari prodded.

"Nightbloom is precious to the fae," she said. "They use it for ceremonies. So they keep the places where the nightbloom grow secret. Protected."

Akari nodded and peered at the map again. "I know. Which is why I was surprised Sera said there was some out there. If there was a cache of nightbloom there, wouldn't people know about it?"

"Some people might," Yoshimi said, but her meaning was clear. The fae might know about the nightbloom on the mountain, but humans wouldn't.

Akari ran her fingers over the map. It was crudely drawn. Primitive. It was also browned with age and the edges frayed.

"Sera is friendly with the fae communities," Akari said. "She probably got this from them."

"But why would she give it to you?" Yoshimi asked. "You're not fae. The fae wouldn't take kindly to you stumbling through one of their nightbloom fields."

"Takeo is fae," Akari reminded Yoshimi.

"True," Yoshimi said as she cleared the dishes from the table. "But I doubt she is sending you out there for his benefit."

Akari sighed and put a few more items into her pack. "What are you trying to say?"

"Just...be careful," Yoshimi said. She ushered Elwin off to collect his gear, so they could head back to the school for afternoon classes. "That mountain will not be without protection."

Akari bit into an apple as she headed out the door. "Thanks for the heads-up," she said. "I'll bring you back a flower."

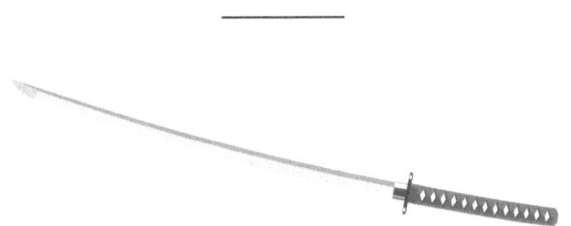

8

*A*s she approached Takeo, she thought she saw a hint of smile cross his face before he quickly pushed it away.

"You were nearly late," he said, heading out of town.

"But not actually late," she corrected. "I was talking to Elwin, and he said something interesting about the nightbloom. I was wondering if you knew of any faeish legends about them."

He shrugged his pack higher up on his shoulders. "What do you mean?" he asked.

"I don't know," she said. She walked a little faster to keep up with him. "He recited a poem about the nightbloom. I can't remember all the words, but it ended with something about 'she' is waiting where the nightbloom grows."

"Who is she?" Takeo asked.

"I asked Elwin, but he didn't know," she said. They turned off the main road and headed up a trail into the woods and up a hill.

Takeo was quiet for a few minutes. Akari thought he was just concentrating on the road when he suddenly piped up. "Oh, I know this haiku," he said.

"Where the nightbloom grow
Is where my heart will find you
She waits there also."

"Yes!" Akari said, a little too excitedly. "That's the one." They exited the town and headed off into the woods toward the mountain.

"I think it is just a poem," Takeo said. "I don't think it means anything."

"Have you ever wondered who the 'she' in the poem is?" Akari asked, her legs already starting to burn a little. She looked up the mountain, and it hit her for the first time just how tall it was. She looked back, and it practically towered over Nasu. She wondered why she had never hiked it before. It would be a good place to hold training missions of all types, and it was so close. Usually if she wanted to go hiking, she would head to a different mountain to the south, a few miles away. She would have to start hiking here instead.

"Not really," he said, his eyes watching the trail ahead as it rose up the mountain. "I guess I always thought it was a romantic poem. That 'she' is a waiting lover."

"Makes sense, I guess," Akari said. "I know the nightbloom is said to have aphrodisiac powers."

Takeo laughed, probably for the first time. "I think anything mystical is said to have aphrodisiac powers."

Akari went over to the side of the trail and picked up a long branch she could use as a walking stick. "That is probably true," she said.

"Yoshimi also had a few things to say. Concerns, I guess," Akari said.

"Did she?" Takeo asked. He didn't seem to be exerting himself at all as he went up the mountain.

"Just that the fae are protective of the nightbloom, since they use them in rituals," she said. Takeo didn't respond. "She just said we should be careful. If the fae know the nightbloom are out here, they might be guarded in some way."

"True," he said, leaping over some fallen tree trunks. Akari did her best to jump over them, but she ended up crawling as gracefully as a slug. "But it's not like they will come at us with pitchforks if they see us. They might just try to send us away without letting you pick one for Sera."

"It's just weird that Sera sent us out here," Akari panted. "The last thing we need are more tensions with the fae."

"It does seem like a waste of time," he admitted. "We need to be looking for the shadow monster."

"We finally agree on something," Akari said.

"I guess this building teamwork mission is working then," Takeo said with a smirk.

"Just don't tell Sera," Akari said. "She'd never let me live it down."

*T*hey walked for many hours, until dusk, following the map deeper into the forest and up the mountain.

"We should camp here," Takeo said when they came to a cave. "This looks like a safe place to spend the night."

"Does it?" she asked, peering into the dark hole. "What if someone—or something—already lives there?"

"Are you afraid of the dark, Akari?" he asked playfully.

Wow, first a laugh, now a joke? Takeo appeared to be letting his guard down. Maybe the brisk climb had been good for them.

"Of course not," Akari said. She pulled out a box of matches, searching for kindling she could use to make a torch. "But with so many angry demons wandering around, I don't want to risk disturbing something that could kill us in our sleep."

Takeo nodded and handed Akari a short, stout branch. She wound some leaves around it and lit it with a match from her pack, which she then left outside the cave along with Takeo's bag.

"You are right," he said. "We should be extra careful. No one is expecting us back until tomorrow night. If we went missing, no help would come soon enough."

"Geeze," Akari said as she stepped into the cave. "Thanks for the comfort."

"My pleasure," he said, and she wasn't sure if he was joking or serious.

As she stepped into the cavern, it quickly became apparent it was neither deep nor inhabited. It was more of an outcropping than a proper cave.

"We can sleep here," Takeo said. He headed back out to grab their packs.

Akari held her torch aloft and scrutinized the space. On the ground, she saw bits of white rock. She kicked them with her feet, and they sounded...hollow. She bent down to pick them up and noticed they were porous.

"Bones," she said, but then remembered Takeo wasn't there. The ground was littered with the crushed remains of bones. The pieces were too small to identify what kind of animal they had come from. She looked up, but didn't see any owls or bats, which could indicate that they had come from small animals like rats or rabbits.

She stood and walked closer to the back wall. As her eyes adjusted, she realized there were old, faded images painted there. The paint was faint, and chipped away in places, but she saw what looked like small children with shaggy hair running with long sticks.

"What's that?" Takeo asked, and Akari nearly jumped out of her skin.

"Geeze! You really need to learn to make more noise when you walk," she said, gripping her chest.

"Sorry," he said. "I'll try to remember to stomp toward you. Anyway, what are you looking at?"

"Just some old cave drawings," she said, holding her torch back up. "What do you think they are? Anything we should be concerned about?"

"Such primitive drawings could be anything," he said. "They could be real, or they could just be interpretations of something that couldn't be explained. Or the artist could have just been really, really bad."

"You're no help at all," she said. She pushed past him and went to set up camp.

*T*hey built a fire in the middle of the cave and used it to boil water. They used the water to clean themselves off a bit since they had gotten rather warm and dirty on their hike.

Akari offered Takeo some of her tsukemono, and he offered her some of his mikan chuhai. The alcohol content was low, but enough to help her relax. She hated sleeping outside. It left her feeling exposed, vulnerable. She hoped the chuhai would calm her enough to get a bit of rest.

"The rest of the hike to the ruins tomorrow looks quite arduous," Akari said as she examined the map. "Very steep, but not as far as we walked today."

Takeo reached out, and she handed him the paper. "So, what is the real reason you think Sera sent us out here?" he asked.

"What do you mean?" Akari asked. She poked at the fire with a stick, sending sparks floating up to the roof of the cave.

"It's just a hike, so far at least," he said, handing the map back to her. "Nothing to encourage teambuilding."

She took it back and folded it into her pocket. "Who knows," she said. "Maybe we will find out tomorrow."

They sat in an awkward silence for a moment, with Akari unsure what to ask to continue the conversation. Thankfully, Takeo finally spoke up.

"Your sister," he said, not taking his eyes off the fire. "Why does she work with the fae?"

Akari shrugged. "She has always been drawn to them, their people, their culture. She made friends more easily with fae kids than human ones when we were little. She loves their music, their art, their language. The fae communities here have always been welcoming of her, so she has been more than happy to work with them and help them as much as she can."

"She is a good woman," he said, and Akari felt a little tug of annoyance. It irked her that he was praising her sister, which she then realized was stupid. Of course her sister was a good person who did good work. She had said so many times herself. She had defended Yoshimi's relationship to the fae more times than she could count. So why was it upsetting her for Takeo to say it now? She had a feeling she knew why, but she didn't want to give voice to it.

Takeo must have noticed Akari wasn't responding because he asked, "What about you? Do you feel drawn to the fae culture?"

"I didn't have a choice of what to do in my life," she said. "So it doesn't matter. I'm Sword Kissed. I have to battle demons and keep all people—human and fae—safe."

"It is a noble calling," Takeo said.

"I just wish it had been more of a choice," Akari said. "I just feel like...my life is a job. It's not something I hate, but I don't love it either. Yoshimi, her life, her job, it is not easy. The humans... they don't support her, and she often feels like an outcast. But she loves her job, her kids, her fae friends. Despite the difficulties, she is happy."

"But you are not happy?" Takeo asked.

"I exist," Akari said. "And that has to be enough for me."

Takeo stood and moved to Akari's side of the fire, sitting close to her. "That cannot be enough," he said. "How can you fight if you don't have something to fight for?"

"I fight to protect the people," Akari said. "I fight for them."

Takeo shook his head. "But if you died, would you be sad? Would you miss this world? The people?"

Akari dipped her head, staring into the fire, yet she felt cold. She felt her eyes well with tears.

"If I were dead, what would it matter?" she asked, trying to turn his questions into a joke. It would hurt too much if he was serious.

"You know that's not what I mean," he said.

"No," she finally admitted.

Takeo nodded. "I see the hopelessness in your eyes," he said. "I saw it the moment we met. If you don't care if you live or die, are you really fighting at full strength?"

Akari paused for a moment. She had felt...listless for so long. Like she was only drifting through life. She was the best of the Sword Kissed fighters. She had never met a demon she could not defeat. And she had no one in her life who needed her. Yes, Yoshimi would miss her if she died, but she didn't need her to survive like a child. Yoshimi would be fine.

"Maybe this is why Sera pushes me so hard," Akari said. "She knows I am not the best fighter I could be."

Takeo nodded. "But Sera doesn't seem to see what you are missing. She knows you could be better, but not how to help you reach the next level in your fighting skills other than to push you.

Which seems to only make you more resentful of your teacher and your life."

"But you know?" Akari asked. "You know what I'm missing to make me a better fighter, even though I've only known you for like a day?"

"Maybe," he said. "I think you are missing true purpose. Your reason for living. Fighting demons is a job, not the reason you wake up every day."

"So what could my reason be?" Akari asked.

"Anything," Takeo said excitedly. "If you could do anything, what would it be? Would you paint seascapes? Cook delicious foods? Find a way to bridge the Hollows?"

"I...I don't know," Akari said, feeling a little excitement build in her chest. "I've never given it much thought. Bridge the Hollows? That would be...incredible. Is anyone even working on that?"

"There are scientists and magic wielders in Ryu who have been working on finding a way to travel from one Hollow to the others for years, but they have not made much progress. They do have radios. Old decrepit things from before the Great Divide that somehow still work. They use them to contact people with radios in other Hollows."

"That's amazing," Akari said. "Why does no one talk about this? I knew about the radios, but not that they were using them regularly to collect news and information. I've never read anything in the paper about news from other Hollows."

Takeo shrugged. "I suppose it doesn't matter. Until we can travel to another Hollow, who cares what is happening out there?"

"Is it true that the fae once lived in their own Hollow?" Akari asked. "Back when the world was One?"

"Well, I don't know that it was true," he said. "I've never been there, and I've never known a fae who has been there. We call it the fae realm, though, not Hollow. There are some who want to go back there as well. But it was shut off to us, just as the rest of the world was locked away, in the Great Divide."

"That must be very sad for the fae," she said. "To be locked away from their homeland."

Takeo nodded. "I think it is why many fae don't fight back against the segregation here. They don't feel they truly belong here anyway."

"What about you?" Akari asked. "Do you feel like you belong here?"

"Yes," he said. "And no. You could say I'm of two minds about it."

They both laughed, and Akari started to feel at ease with Takeo for the first time. She wanted to lay her head on his shoulder, entwine her fingers with his, but she couldn't. They were partners. It wouldn't be appropriate as workmates. She thought maybe the chuhai was having a bit of an effect on her as well.

"And what about your family?" she finally asked. "How did that even happen? Your parents? That must be a beautiful story."

"It was..." he said, gazing into his drink. "It was."

"That's not fair," she said. "You know all about my sister and my...lacking a reason to live and fight. Tell me more about you."

He lifted his head, staring into her eyes. "Maybe someday," he said with a small smile.

"Oh, come on!" she said a little more loudly than she intended. "You can't..."

He placed his lips on hers, and she stopped talking. Her eyes were wide in surprise, but she noticed his were closed. He opened his mouth a bit, sucking her bottom lip into the warm wetness. She felt a quiver in her belly, and she let her eyes close, too. She felt the heat from the fire, the chuhai, his kiss all radiating through her. He reached up and stroked her cheek, and she placed her hand on his arm and kissed him back. His lips were soft, and she could feel the muscles in his biceps.

She still wanted to know more about him, his family, his history. Who was this strange man who walked between worlds?

She needed to know him, and yet, in that kiss, she knew enough.

Maybe Sera had been right to send them into the woods alone after all.

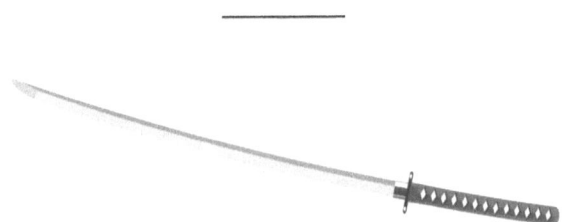

9

*S*akura, sakura...

Akari stirred fitfully. She knew she was sleeping. She could feel the heaviness of her body and could see only black. But she could hear someone singing to her the song of her mother. But it was not her mother's voice.

Blossoms on the trees
Blossoms in the sky
Are you a human
Or are you a fairy?
Sakura, sakura of mine...

Akari felt herself stand, but she still could not see anything, as if she was moving in a dream.

"Hello?" she called. No one responded. She tried to take a step forward, but her foot felt as if it were stuck in deep mud. She reached down and tried to pull her foot loose, but not only did it not budge, she was sinking deeper!

She struggled to lift her feet, but she felt wetness creeping up her clothes, drenching her and pulling her down.

"Help," she exclaimed.

*Sakura...sakura...*she heard the voice reply, but still she could see nothing.

"Help me," she cried as she sank up to her neck. "Takeo!"

Her eyes sprung open. She gasped. She had been sleeping. It was all just a terrible dream. Then she realized she was drenched. *Oh my gods!* she thought. *Was I so scared I wet myself?* She pushed herself up and saw the whole floor of the cave was completely wet. Takeo sat on his mat on the other side of their now-dead fire. He was wearing a straw hat in an attempt to protect himself, but it wasn't doing him any good. Over him was a small cloud, and rain was falling from it, soaking him and spreading across the cave floor.

"What's going on?" Akari asked as she jumped to her feet.

Takeo spit water from his mouth and tried to wipe his face, but the rain kept falling. "That's what I would like to know," he said. "I woke up to this. I thought at first there was a hole in the cave ceiling or something. But when I moved, the rain followed me. It didn't take me long to figure out the rain was...stalking me. But I haven't found the source yet."

Akari did her best to move their things away from the water, but it was too late. Everything was wet. She went outside, and Takeo followed her. The sun was starting to rise, so she at least had some light to help her look to find the cause of Takeo's rain cloud.

"Did you hear anything?" she asked. "Any movement or words being uttered?"

He shook his head, sending rain drops flying. "No, nothing," he said. "I only woke up when I thought you had dropped a bucket of water on my head."

She stood in a puddle of water, her shoes soaked through. Akari groaned. She was never going to get dry.

"Just go stand over there," she said, waving him away. "I can't focus with you dripping everywhere."

Takeo rolled his eyes as he walked away.

"Who is there?" Akari called. She wasn't sure anyone was, but there had to be a magical source to the cloud. Either someone was actively creating it, or they created it and then left. She hoped whoever made it was still around. She wouldn't have any idea how to banish the rain cloud on her own.

"I am Sword Kissed Tanaka," she said, holding up her empty hands. "I mean you no harm. Show yourself."

Still nothing. She shrugged at Takeo. She noticed the water running off him wasn't flowing down, toward the cave, but uphill toward the woods. The water was probably flowing to whoever was creating it. Akari walked back down the trail a bit, away from where the water was. She then looped around, hoping to come up behind whoever might be watching them and catch the person by surprise.

She had to move slowly and carefully since the woods were quite overgrown here, and everywhere she stepped there were fallen leaves and broken branches. She got as close to where she had seen the water flowing as possible, but she still couldn't see anything through the trees. She drew her sword and took a deep breath. Then she leaped in the direction of where the person must be hiding.

"Ah-ha," she shouted.

"Ahh!" a woman screamed. Akari felt a bucket of water fall on her, and not stop. Raising her head, she saw a cloud over her now, raining a torrent.

The woman who had screamed was holding an umbrella, but she also was dripping wet. She was small and thin with pale skin and black hair.

"I'm so sorry," the woman said. She waved her hand, and the rain cloud dissipated.

It was apparent the woman was not a threat. Akari sheathed her sword and squeezed her hair out. "Who are you?"

"Forgive me," she said. "My name is Ameonna. I am—"

"A rain sprite," Takeo said. He approached from the other side, rain still falling on him.

Sprites were a sort of hill folk. Small creatures of myth and magic that were not considered demons. Some people thought they were a sort of fae, but more magic than human.

"Yes," Ameonna said. "I was only trying to protect you, Tanaka-san."

"Protect me?" Akari asked. "From what?"

"From him," she said, glaring at Takeo.

"Why do I need protecting from him?" Akari asked, suddenly alarmed. Had he done something in the night? Something Akari wasn't aware of? Her hand instinctively went to the hilt of her sword.

"I saw him...kissing you," Ameonna said shyly. "I wasn't sure if it was what you wanted."

"Ah, yes," Takeo said, spitting water as he spoke. "A water sprite and a guiding spirit for women. She leads the souls of women who have died by drowning to the afterlife."

"And protecting living women when I can," Ameonna said proudly. "But not many people come through here anymore."

"It's all right, Ameonna," Akari said. "He's not a threat. The kiss was welcome."

Takeo smirked, and Akari felt her face go hot. "Well...I mean...you know...he doesn't need to be punished for it anyway," Akari clarified clumsily.

"As you wish, Tanaka-san," Ameonna said. She waved her hand, and the rain cloud over Takeo faded away.

Takeo lifted his head and took off the straw hat. "Finally," he said with a relieved sigh.

"Thank you, Ameonna," Akari said with a bow. "I know you meant no harm."

"Well, we few creatures of the hills, we must do what we can to protect the land and the people who live here," Ameonna said.

"What do you mean?" Akari asked. "Where are the other hill creatures?"

Ameonna gripped her chest and shook her head. "Gone," she said sadly. "The blackness, it took them away, one by one."

"The blackness?" Takeo asked. "You mean like a shadow?"

"Not exactly," Ameonna said. "This blackness is in the earth. We hill spirits, we are born from the earth, one and the same. The earth, it is poisoned. If the earth dies, we die."

"What is causing this blackness?" Akari asked. "This poison?"

"Chiyoko," Ameonna said. "She is sick."

Akari nodded. Chiyoko Hollow was another name for the world in which they now lived, their little piece of it. It was just another way of saying the world was poisoned.

"What can you tell us about the mountain?" Akari asked, pulling out her now-drenched map, which she now realized was not an old parchment, but vellum, which was why the rain did not destroy it. "We are supposed to be looking for ruins and a cave with nightblooms."

Ameonna reached for the map. "Let me see this," she said, examining it closely. "Where did you get this? It is quite old. Fae crafted."

"From my sensei," Akari said. "She is the one who sent us here."

"Without this map," Ameonna said handing it back, "you never would have gotten this far. This mountain, it is protected by fae magic. Humans can't see it without a key or other enchanted item to let them pierce the veil."

At that, it was like a shadow had been lifted from Akari's eyes and she was seeing the mountain clearly for the first time. No wonder she had never noticed its size or gone hiking here before. She literally couldn't see what was right in front of her.

"Did you know about this?" Akari asked Takeo accusingly. "Can you see the...veil or whatever magic is being used?"

Takeo shook his head. "I didn't know I was supposed to be looking for any. I can access fae magic, but only if I know it is there. Since I'm not full fae, it isn't something that works all the time. I have to be deliberate in my use of it."

"This must be why we didn't know there were ruins or caves here," Akari said. "It was shielded by fae magic for some reason. But why? What is so special about these ruins?"

"I guess we will find out when we see them," Takeo said.

"Thank you for your help, Ameonna," Akari said. "But we have a long journey ahead. We should get going."

"Good luck to you, my friends," Ameonna said as she waved them goodbye.

"At least the hill sprites aren't turning evil the way the demons have," Akari said. She headed back to their cave, packed up her wet gear, and hoisted her bag on her back.

"No," Takeo said. "They are just dying."

"It's all connected," Akari said. "The blackness, the shadows. The evil demons, the dying hill folk. I wonder if the other Hollows are facing similar problems."

Takeo did his best to squeeze the excess water out of his clothes and bag as he packed. "It would make sense," he said. "The world is not physically fragmented, only divided by preternatural spheres. If the core of the earth is sick, then every Hollow would be sick as well."

"You said people were able to contact the other Hollows by radio," Akari said while they started back up the trail. "Maybe we can ask them if they have had any success fighting the earth's poison."

"We can try when we get back," Takeo said. He offered Akari his hand to help her climb over some large rocks blocking their path. "I only know of a radio tower back in Ryu, though."

"Sera is an important woman," Akari said. "She knows a lot of people. She can probably reach out to someone for information."

"How well do you know Sera?" Takeo asked. "Does she have any fae blood?"

Akari sighed as she adjusted her pack, which was heavier than it should have been since everything was laden with water. "Sera has been my sensei since my parents realized I was Sword Kissed when I was just a kid. She's been like a third parent to me."

"And?" Takeo asked.

"And what?" Akari asked, having already forgotten what they were talking about.

"Sera," he said. "How well do you know her?"

"She's been my sensei since my parents discovered—"

"You just said that," Takeo interrupted.

"Said what" Akari asked. "Come on. We don't have time for this."

"Come here," he said, taking her hand. "Get the map. Hold it in your hand."

She wasn't sure what he was getting at, but she did as he said.

"Now," he said, steadily gazing into her eyes. "What do you know about Sera?"

"She's my...sensei..." Akari started to say, but then she remembered she had already said that. "She's...I don't know. When I think about it, I don't know anything about her. Where is she from? Who taught her to sword dance? Does she have a family? I feel like I've been wearing blinders for the last fifteen years."

"Like...there's a veil between you?" Takeo asked.

Akari took a step back. It was exactly like that. She had known this mountain was here her whole life, but she had never thought to climb it or ask if there was anything significant on it. It was as though she could see the mountain, but as soon as she looked away, she forgot about it. It never entered her mind she should climb it until she was handed the map and told to.

It was the same with Sera. She had known Sera her whole life, but she had never thought of Sera as having a life outside of their training sessions. It was like she was a ghost who couldn't exist outside the walls of the dojo.

Who was Sera? How did she have this map? What did she know about the fae world? Was she even human?

"Looks like you and Sera are going to have a long chat when we get back," Takeo said with a chuckle as he let go of her hand and headed back up the mountain.

Akari kept walking, but she could feel the scowl that had appeared on her face. She was mad and hurt. She felt as though she had been betrayed, lied to her whole life. Sera knew more than she was letting on, and Akari was going to find out exactly what that was.

Was that why Sera had sent Akari on this training mission? To open her eyes to the fae veil? To see through Sera's lies? But why hadn't Sera simply told her the truth?

Because nothing was ever simple with Sera.

Oh, they would have a chat when she got back. There was no mistake in that.

"Let's forget about Sera for now," Akari said as she squeezed her hands into fists. "We need to keep going and see just what's hidden up here."

She gasped as a tiny stone rolled down the mountain and smacked her in the forehead.

"What the hell?" she asked as she looked up. At first, she didn't see anything, but then she felt Takeo's hand on her shoulder.

"Akari," he said softly. He eyed the woods around them.

Akari followed his gaze, and she finally saw them.

They were surrounded.

10

*T*hey were surrounded by demons.

Dozens of carved demonic faces on traditional tribal masks stared down at them. They were painted blue or white and adorned with horns and fangs. Their eyes and mouths were painted blood red. The creatures were standing above them, holding the higher ground.

For a moment, all stood still. Then one of the demons let out a terrifying shriek. It was as if it were a signal for all the monsters to yell out war cries and hold spears aloft. Akari drew her sword, and Takeo nocked an arrow in his bow.

The demons threw rocks and sticks down on Akari and Takeo, and they did their best to bat them away. They backed down the mountain a bit to try and gain a better fighting advantage. Akari couldn't fight them from where she was. She needed to be face to face with her opponent. But Takeo loosed an arrow. The demon he was aiming at was able to dodge, the arrow just skirting by his head. He let an arrow fly at another one, but the demon used a shield to block it.

"Damn it," Takeo cursed. "I can't get a good shot from down here."

"Come on," Akari said, heading back down the trail. "I think I saw another way up the mountain. It's not on the map, but..."

The demons hooted and hollered, and then Akari felt the ground beneath her feet shake. Takeo clearly felt it, too. They looked back up the mountain and saw a huge boulder rolling toward them.

Akari let out a gasp. She tried to step out of the way, but she knew she was too slow. She was going to be crushed! She closed her eyes and braced for impact.

Something slammed into her side, pushing her flat against the mountain and out of the way at the last second. She opened her eyes. Takeo had her pinned safely against the mountain wall.

"I didn't know fae had super speed," she said.

"Among other things," he replied, breathing hard, anger on his face. After making sure no other boulders were coming, he unsheathed both of his daggers. With monkey-like agility, he grabbed onto the trees lining the trail and zipped up the mountain toward the demons.

"Ay-yi!" one of the creatures yelled as Takeo knocked it down. Takeo kicked another creature below the knee, and it fell and began to cry. A creature in a terrifying blue mask ran away screaming as Takeo advanced toward it.

Confusion crossed Takeo's face. These weren't hard and fast warriors like they first thought. They were scared little critters of some sort.

Another demon ran at him, holding a spear aloft, but Takeo simply placed his hand on the creature's forehead to keep him from advancing.

Akari looked around and saw that several of the creatures had gathered around her. She raised her sword, but they were not attacking. They seemed to observing her curiously. She sheathed her sword and held her hands up in surrender.

"I have no wish to harm you," she said. "I am a Sword Kissed. A protector. I am here to help Chiyoko."

The demons turned to one another and made little chirping noises.

"What's going on?" Takeo called.

"I think they are trying to decide if they are going to kill us or not," Akari replied.

Takeo pushed the creature that was still swinging a stick at him away, causing it to fall, and he descended the mountain to stand at Akari's side.

"We are here to help you," Takeo said, also holding up his hands. "We are friends of the hill folk. We want to heal the poisoned land."

The creatures grew very excited, beginning to chirp even more loudly. Finally, one of the creatures approached Takeo and took off his mask. What they saw looked like a cross between a small child and a bear cub.

"They are kappa," Takeo said with a sigh of relief.

"What is a kappa?" Akari asked as the rest of the creatures took off their masks.

"We are the children of the forest," one of the creatures said. "The last of Chiyoko's protectors."

"Protectors of the earth," Takeo said with a laugh. "We are here to help you. We want to help Chiyoko as well."

"So we are just going to forget they tried to smash us with a giant stone?" Akari said quietly. "Okay."

"Well, they didn't know why we were here," Takeo said. "Like Ameonna. Who knows how long it has been since people last came here through the veil."

"No," one of the other kappa said. "No people. Only kappa. Only hill folk."

Takeo nodded. "I understand. But Chiyoko is very sick, right?" The kappa all nodded their heads in agreement. "My friend and I, we were sent to help Chiyoko. To find out why she is sick and to heal her."

"Chiyoko sick long time," another one of the kappa said. "Sick all time."

"Chiyoko has been sick the whole time?" Akari asked. "How is that possible?"

"Chiyoko eat the sick," another kappa said. "Chiyoko get sicker."

Akari shook her head and whispered to Takeo, "This isn't making any sense. We need to find those ruins and caves."

Takeo nodded. "Little friends, can you tell us where we can find the ruins?"

The kappa looked at one another with confusion.

"Ruins," Takeo tried again. "Old buildings."

The kappa chirped amongst themselves and shook their heads.

"Falling-down place," one of the kappa finally said. "You want to go to falling-down place?"

"Umm, maybe," Takeo said. "That is as good a place as any to start."

The kappa said something to the others, and then they all chirped and nodded happily.

"Let's go! Let's go," they all started saying as they made their way up the hill. They grabbed Takeo's and Akari's hands, pulling them along as though they were old friends.

They had not traveled far when they saw what was left of a gold statue. It appeared feminine in form, but the head and arms were missing.

"Rasha," Akari said, reading the plaque at the statue's base. "I've never heard of her. Have you?"

Takeo shook his head.

"Mother," one of the kappa said, pointing to Rasha.

"Your mother?" Akari asked, surprised she had never heard the name before if she was some sort of mother goddess. World

Mythology had been one of her favorite classes back in school, and she knew the deities from China and Greece rather well.

"All mother," the kappa said.

Akari shook her head. The little critter must have been mistaken, or perhaps the hill folk had developed their own mythology.

"Well whoever she was, hopefully it means we are traveling in the right direction," Akari said.

"I wonder what happened to her," Takeo replied.

"Hopefully we won't find out," Akari said uneasily. She wasn't sure they could trust these kappa creatures. They seemed sweet and innocent now, but they had certainly tried to kill them and not just scare them away only minutes before.

"There!" one of the kappa finally called out as she pointed up ahead. "Falling-down place."

Akari saw the remains of an old wooden archway. It had been painted red at one time, but the paint had faded and chipped away. At that moment, Akari remembered the paintings on the wall of the cave where they had spent the night. The little creatures she saw in the cave paintings must have been the kappa. She had a feeling that whoever built the archway probably made the cave paintings as well, or they were at least from the same time. It looked as though it predated the Great Divide.

Beyond the archway was an old temple. The grounds around the temple were completely covered with knee-high grass, as if no one had walked through it for ages. And dotted throughout the grounds were large cherry blossom trees, the blooms of which were delicately falling and being scattered by the wind.

Sakura...sakura...

Akari gasped. "Did you hear that?" she asked.

"Hear what?" Takeo asked.

Akari shook her head. She must have only thought the words to the song when she saw the sakura—cherry blossom—petals falling.

"Careful. Careful," the kappa said, putting their fingers to their lips in a shushing motion. "Must be careful. Must be quiet."

"Why don't you kappa stay here?" Akari said to them. "We will inspect the...falling-down place."

The kappa nodded in agreement.

Akari took a deep breath and drew her sword.

"Expecting a fight?" Takeo asked as he pulled out his daggers, twirling them in his fingers.

"It pays to be prepared," Akari said as they started to cross the yard toward the front door of the temple.

The stairs squeaked as they took the two steps up to the temple porch. They looked around, but they did not see anything to cause alarm. The kappa kept their distance, crowding the gate as they watched eagerly.

Akari saw no reason to delay. She turned to the temple door, which was already hanging open a crack.

"Are you ready?" she asked Takeo.

Takeo nodded.

Akari opened the door.

11

*A*kari gasped. There was a large open room, in the center of which was a huge statue. Akari took a tenuous step inside. The floor creaked, and she hesitated, but there seemed to be no traps or other dangers. She opened the door wide to let in more light, and cherry blossoms blew across the floor. Takeo stepped inside behind her.

She walked up to the statue. It was of a woman in flowing robes at least ten feet tall. She was reclining on a flat stone and gazing at Akari with a gentle smile on her face. Her hair was piled atop her head in a very old style. Around her were carvings of little animals, such as rabbits and fawns. Behind her was a cherry blossom tree with the branches and blossoms hanging over her. In her right hand, draped casually over her knee, was a katana.

Akari noticed that the katana was not to scale and appeared small in the woman's large hand. She took a step closer to get a better look. The blade shimmered in the light. The katana was not carved, but had been forged from steel, a real katana.

Sakura...

"What did you say?" Akari asked, turning to Takeo.

He shook his head, not taking his eyes off what he was looking at across the room. "Nothing. I was just looking at these paintings."

Akari followed his gaze to the wall. All four walls were decorated with ornate paintings. The pane they were looking at was terrifying. It showed the land of Chiyoko in flames. The people were running and screaming, and the earth had been ripped asunder. Demons of all sorts were pouring out of the rift and attacking the humans.

"By the gods," Akari whispered. "It's depicting the Great Divide." She wasn't sure how she knew this. She had never seen anything like it before, but she knew. And Takeo nodded in agreement. She started to move to the next panel, but Takeo gently took her hand.

"Let's start at the beginning," he said. He pulled her to the panel nearest the door.

The first panel showed not just Chiyoko, but the whole world as one. It depicted people—humans, not fae—living their lives, farming, fishing, marrying, building homes, caring for the animals. They seemed to be happy. They were all smiling, playing music, hugging their children. It appeared the world was perfect.

She knew they were humans because they all had pale skin and black hair. Legend said that at one time, people in Chiyoko —well, back when it had been called Japan—had people of various shades as well. Humans could be white, black, brown, red, and more. And their hair came in many varieties as well. She had always wondered what she would have looked like with yellow hair. But even then, the number of people with these different features was extremely small compared to the overall population. After Chiyoko Hollow formed and the people were cut off from the rest of the world, the people with yellow hair or brown skin seemed to fade away. Akari had never seen a human who didn't have the same skin and hair color she herself had.

They moved to the next panel. This one also appeared to show the world, but the continents were shaped differently and the overall color scheme was different. While the first painting seemed to be bathed in sunlight, this one was more green, as if the whole world was a luscious garden. The people were clearly fae—they were in many different shapes and colors—and they too were depicted as living normally, happily. But they were also shown using magic, with sparks coming from fingertips or children apparently talking to animals.

She thought it was interesting there were no demons, not even what she would call "good demons," the innocent tricksters or protectors that existed alongside the dangerous demons. There were no sprites or hill folk either. She wondered what that meant.

Takeo was gritting his teeth and his eyes were glistening.

"It's home," he finally said. "It's the fae realm. I've never... never seen a rendition of it. There are none alive who remember it."

"It is beautiful," Akari said, squeezing his hand.

He nodded and gave her a small smile.

They moved to the next panel. This one was half fae realm and half Chiyoko. The fae and the humans appeared to be living in both realms.

"It looks like the veil between worlds had disappeared," Akari said. "And humans and fae lived together in both worlds."

"I wonder how that happened," Takeo said. The panels had no words, only images, so they had to do their best to interpret the story based solely on the paintings.

The next painting was rimmed in red, and the humans and fae were fighting each other. The world was dark, the earth scorched and the animals dead.

"How terrible," Akari said. "It looks like the fae and humans started fighting, but there is no explanation about how they came to be enemies."

"Maybe it doesn't matter," Takeo said. "There could not be a cause great enough to justify this kind of death and destruction."

Akari nodded. The reasons for the fighting were lost to time, and they would probably never find out the true history behind it. But it didn't matter. They needed to find out how to fix Chiyoko now.

The next panel was the one they had seen originally, with the earth ripped open and about to crumble. This was the first panel that showed demons, and they were pouring out of the rift. Akari surmised this was the origins of the demons in the world, which didn't surprise her.

The next panel, though, showed a beautiful woman. She was weeping for the earth, and she held thirteen smaller women in her arms.

"This looks like a mother and her daughters," Akari said. "She seems frightened."

Akari squinted and noticed there were kanji characters drawn on the flowing gowns of the mother and each of the daughters. It had been many years since she had studied traditional kanji, but she could make out just enough.

"Rasha..." Akari read on the mother. "That's the same name on the statue outside."

"It sounds like a fae name," Takeo said.

Akari nodded. "Crystal," she read on one of the daughters. "That must be the name of this daughter. Solana...Chiyoko!" She looked back at the statue. It looked just like the daughter labeled Chiyoko in the painting. "If they are names, then Chiyoko isn't just the name of our Hollow," Akari said. "It is the name of this daughter. Her name is Chiyoko."

"Then what happened?" Takeo asked, rushing to the next panel.

In the next panel, the mother was burying her daughters in the earth. And from them, bursts of light were pouring forth.

"It looks like she buried her daughters in the earth, and that is what created the Hollows," Akari said. "The light from the daughters stitched the earth back together."

The rifts in the earth were smaller in this image, and the demons that had poured out were retreating.

The next, and final, image showed Chiyoko buried in Chiyoko Hollow under a cherry blossom tree, her face serene and a sword in her hand. The world was healed, and the demons sealed up. The humans and fae were once again living side by side, but it didn't look as peaceful. They were working, but not celebrating, playing.

"So...what happened?" Takeo asked, clearly disappointed there wasn't another image. "Chiyoko, and all the daughters, were buried in the earth by a powerful fae goddess in order to repair the world. It seemed to have worked initially. So what is happening now? Why is the land poisoned and the demons returning?"

Akari ran her fingers over the buried demons in the painting. "Who knows," she said. "The demons weren't destroyed. They were just buried along with Chiyoko. Maybe one of them infected her."

Takeo nodded. "Yes," he said. "Remember what the water sprite said. She said Chiyoko was sick. I thought she was speaking metaphorically, saying the world was sick, which we already knew..."

"But she might have meant it literally," Akari said, completing his thought. "She meant Chiyoko, the buried daughter, was sick."

"Exactly!" Takeo said, excited, but then he turned somber. "But what now? These panels, this temple, they were built when the world seemed to have been healed. They don't say what to do if Chiyoko got infected by the demons."

Akari sighed. He was right. While her heart felt light at

knowing what happened in the past, she was still at a loss for what to do now.

"She certainly loved cherry blossoms," Akari said. In the images and around the statue, cherry blossoms featured predominantly. She remembered the cherry blossoms around the temple. Then she remembered that cherry blossoms could be found all through Chiyoko. They were a source of national pride, and many communities held cherry blossom festivals every year.

"Actually, the creatures, the demons," Akari said. "Have you heard them singing about cherry blossoms?"

Takeo looked confused. "The demons? Singing? No, I haven't heard that."

Akari paced. "Every time I get near a demon, they recite a song that my mother used to sing to me.

> "Sakura, sakura,
> Blossoms on the trees
> Blossoms in the sky
> Are you a human
> Or are you a fairy?
> Sakura, sakura of mine.

"But why? Why would the demons sing that song?" she asked.

"Your mother used to sing it to you?" Takeo asked. Akari nodded. "That's an old fae song. All fae mothers sing it to their children before bed."

"But my mother wasn't fae," Akari said.

"Are you sure?" Takeo asked, raising an eyebrow.

"I...I always thought I was sure," Akari said. But she never thought Sera was fae either until now. She rubbed her forehead. Everything she ever thought she knew was being called into questions. "No, she had to be human," Akari finally decided. "My grandparents were human. All Sword Kissed are human."

"Yet, your mother used to sing you a fae lullaby, you possess powers beyond a normal human, and the demons have been calling to you using the symbol of a buried fae goddess," Takeo said, growing agitated.

"What are you saying?" Akari asked.

Takeo shook his head. He didn't have to say it.

Akari was part fae.

12

*A*kari reached up and touched her ear. Obviously, it was round, not pointed like a fae, like Takeo's ears. Her ears had always been round like a human's. They wouldn't have suddenly changed shape just because she had learned something new. She began to pace. She was so confused.

"There are worse things in the world than discovering you are part fae," Takeo said harshly.

"I know that," Akari said. "I'm not..." She sighed. "I'm not upset about being part fae. I'm just a little overwhelmed, I guess. I mean, how is it possible? If there was fae blood in me, it would have to go way, way back. As I said, as far as I know, all my ancestors were human."

"As far as you know," Takeo repeated. "Maybe someone had a fae lover at some point."

"I really don't want to imagine that Baba cheated on Jiji with a hot fae dude," Akari said with weak laugh. "Besides, it must not have been a secret. If my mother sang me that fae song, she must have known the truth."

"Not necessarily," Takeo said. "If you mother sang it to you without knowing the history, maybe her mother sang it to her without knowing why. And so on and so on. It has just been passed down from mothers to daughters for...who knows how long. All the way back to Chiyoko."

Akari shook her head. "I need to get back home. Talk to Yoshimi. Maybe she knows something I don't. She is older and has spent more time with the fae. Maybe Okāsan told her something..."

"It is getting late," Takeo said. "We will have to rush back."

"Going downhill will be easier anyway," Akari said as she followed Takeo out. As she turned to close the door to the temple, she saw the light gleam off the sword in Chiyoko's hand. She bowed to the statue.

Thank you, she mouthed. They didn't learn how to defeat the growing threat, or how to heal the sick goddess, but they at least had a more complete picture about what was going on. And Akari might have learned more about herself than she ever could have imagined.

"Will we remember this place after we pass back through the veil?" Akari asked Takeo when they descended the mountain.

"We should," he said. He nimbly leaped over rocks and downed trees. "Once you have seen through the veil, you will always know it's there, so it won't work on you anymore."

"What about other veils?" she asked. Takeo didn't answer. "Takeo," she said more forcefully. "I assume the fae have actually created veils all over Chiyoko to hide things from humans. Will I be able to see through them now?"

"No," he finally said even though he didn't look at her. "No, you shouldn't be able to see through any other veils. Not easily, anyway."

"Should I be worried?" she asked. "About what the fae are hiding? I don't mind if they are hiding their people or their food supplies. But are they hiding anything I should be worried about? Like weapons?"

Takeo sighed. "The fae are not your enemy, Akari. In fact, they might be your family."

"I don't..." She cut herself off and grunted. She then took a deep breath to calm down. "I don't see the fae as my enemy," she said. "But we live in a divided world. Believe me, if humans could stockpile weapons and hide them from the fae, they probably would. People—human and fae—are paranoid like that."

Takeo took a moment to respond. "I don't know of any weapons the fae are hiding," he said. "But they do hide a lot of things from humans. More than you would expect."

Akari shook her head, but didn't speak to Takeo for the rest of their journey down the mountain. She was still too raw, too shaken by what she had learned to be rational. If she kept talking, she was going to say something she would regret.

They made it back down the mountain in record time. They still had to travel a short way through the woods, though. Akari pulled out the map.

"What are you looking for?" Takeo asked.

"I'm wondering where the veil begins," Akari said, looking back up at the mountain. "I just want to make sure I can still see it when we pass through."

Takeo chuckled. "You'll still see it, trust me."

"Why do you think the fae veiled the mountain anyway?" Akari asked. "Why hide the temple, the history, Chiyoko herself, from the humans? Actually, they probably hid it from other fae as well. You didn't know it was there either."

Takeo shrugged. "Who knows? Maybe they thought that the fewer people who knew about it, the longer it would last."

Akari put the map back in her pocket. "I bet I know someone who knows." Takeo raised an eyebrow. "Sera."

Takeo nodded. "She knows more than she is letting on. It would be good for you to question her when we get back."

As they exited the woods, Akari was starting to feel winded. It had been a long couple of days, and Akari's mind was racing.

There was still so much to do, so much for her to learn. She needed to find Sera, but she also wanted to find Yoshimi. Since Yoshimi was the older sister, her memories of their mother were much stronger, clearer. Yoshimi might remember something significant about their heritage. Yoshimi also associated with the local fae more. Perhaps she had heard rumors, old stories, things that she didn't give much credence to at the time but in light of new information might make more sense.

She was so distracted she nearly didn't see the sword as it came down on her, cutting right in front of her face. Her eyes went wide and she took a step back, quickly drawing her sword.

"Endo!" Akari cried. Endo had turned from Akari and brought her sword hilt down on the back of Takeo's neck, knocking him out cold and sending him to the ground. Akari drew her sword.

"Give me the map," Endo said, but her voice was not right. It was deep and dark.

Akari assumed a fighting stance. "What map?" she asked.

"The map Sera gave you," Endo said. "Give it to me."

They circled each other. Akari figured there was no point in playing stupid. Endo knew all about the map. Akari didn't know why Endo wanted it, but if she thought the best way to get it from Akari was to fight her for it instead of asking, she couldn't want it for any innocent reason.

"No," Akari said.

Endo took a step forward and slashed at Akari. Akari deflected her and stepped back, but not before she had a chance to look Endo in the eyes.

Her eyes were nothing but empty blackness.

"Endo," Akari cried. "What happened to you?"

Endo laughed. "Endo is still here," she said. "But I needed a corporeal form, and Endo was a willing host." The creature stepped forward, then to the side as she slashed left and right.

"What do you mean Endo was a willing host?" Akari asked. "I'll not let you take her."

"What do you care?" Endo asked. "Endo hates you. If not for you, Endo would be Sera's student, the strongest of the Sword Kissed."

"That doesn't matter," Akari said. "I might not be Endo's friend, but I'll be damned if I let some demon use her for pajamas!" Akari went on the attack, running toward the creature. Moving quickly, she tried to unarm it.

Akari wasn't sure how much in charge of Endo's body the creature was, but her sword-fighting techniques were weak. However, she was much stronger physically. Akari used several moves that should have caused the creature to drop her sword, but she held tight.

Endo took a step back and laughed. Her eyes cleared.

"Endo," Akari yelled. "Fight the beast! I will help you."

"Oh, Akari," Endo said, her voice normal. She shook her head. "You just don't get it. I invited the amamehagi into me."

Akari gasped. An amamehagi was a spirit who could inhabit a person's body and cause them to do wicked deeds. While amamehagi were usually nothing more than silly tricksters who caused a person to put dye in the laundry or let a herd of goats free to run through town, Akari was certain this amamehagi had more nefarious intentions if it had been infected like the other demons.

"Endo, what are you doing?" Akari asked. "You let a demon possess you? Why? They are all infected right now. The world is poisoned. That demon is evil!"

"Exactly," Endo said. "The world needs to be cleansed. We Sword Kissed can't do it alone. We need more power, more strength. Give me the map. I know Sera is hiding something from me."

Sera. Akari wondered what exactly Endo had already done. And what did she think she was going to find on the mountain.

There was only the temple. It did tell the history of Chiyoko, but there had been nothing to help her fight the growing evil.

"There was nothing there," Akari said. "It was just a training exercise."

"I'll be the judge of that," Endo said, her eyes going black and her voice changing back to the deep baritone. "Give me the map, Akari. Or I will end you."

If Endo—or her demon—knew about the map and that something was hidden on the mountain, why did she want it so badly? Wouldn't that be enough for her to see through the veil? Maybe not. Takeo did say something about some veils being so strong they needed a key to pierce. Maybe the veil around the mountain was stronger than most, and the map was a key to getting through. She had been skeptical about why the fae would want to hide the temple, but at seeing the darkness in Endo's eyes, she began to understand why they might want to hide something so precious. She wasn't sure what Endo thought she was going to find on the mountain, but she wouldn't put it past Endo's demon to destroy the temple whether she found what she sought or not.

Akari resumed her fighting stance and swiped her sword across her hand, causing it to glow. "I can't wait to see you try," Akari said.

Endo growled and lunged at Akari. For some reason, Endo didn't light her sword. Akari dodged and then deflected Endo's attacks. Endo, like Akari, was Sword Kissed. Her purpose in life was to fight demons like the one inhabiting Endo. Endo probably couldn't light her sword as long as she was possessed by what she was supposed to be fighting. Her light couldn't shine if it was wrapped in darkness. The demon also didn't have Endo's fighting skills.

Akari grunted as Endo slashed haphazardly at her. The demon was not a trained sword dancer, but she was strong and angry, which made her more dangerous than if Akari had simply been fighting a pissed-off Endo.

But fighting demons was what Akari did. It was why she had been chosen. It was why she had been put on this earth. She might not always like it, but she was good at it. She had to stop thinking of Endo as her fellow Sword Kissed, just a fellow rival. She had to think of her as a demon she needed to stop. She needed to be the Sword Kissed she was born to be.

Akari girded her strength and put all her doubts aside. She would spare Endo's life if she could, but her focus had to be on ending the demon inside her. Akari grunted as she launched herself at Endo. She swung her sword in short, quick strikes, forcing Endo to step back, and step back again.

She saw Takeo finally push up, shaking the pain from his head. He locked eyes with Akari, and she was sure the determination on her face told him they needed to show no mercy. He drew his daggers and ran at Endo from behind.

He stabbed Endo in the shoulder, and Endo—and her demon—screamed in pain. It was not a killing blow, but one that would make fighting back nearly impossible.

Endo gasped as the demon, a shadow beast, leaped free from her body. The creature should have appeared as a person wearing a straw costume, but this creature had most likely been completely taken over by the poison that had infected Chiyoko. Endo crumpled to the ground and dropped her sword. She held her injured arm close to her chest.

"You bastard!" Endo yelled, but whether she was talking to Takeo for injuring her or the demon for abandoning her, Akari wasn't sure. And she didn't have time to find out. She kept her eye on the demon as it circled around her. Akari did not give the demon time to recover. She quickly thrust her sword through the middle of the beast.

"No!" Endo screamed as though she were the one in pain.

The demon screeched as well. It flew back to Endo and enveloped her in its smoke.

"Get away from her," Akari yelled. She ran at it with her sword. But as she approached, the smoke cleared.

Endo was gone.

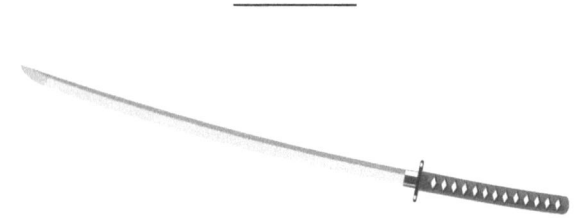

13

"What the hell just happened?" Akari asked as she tried to catch her breath.

Takeo shook his head and sheathed his daggers. "Nothing good. We need to get back to town. If Endo was able to be possessed, who knows what else the demons have been doing."

"I just don't understand it," Akari said. "She is Sword Kissed. We are supposed to fight the demons. But it sounded like she had *willingly* allowed herself to be possessed."

"I don't pretend to know anything about the ways of the Sword Kissed," Takeo said. "But Endo is just like any other person, someone capable of good and bad decisions."

Akari shook her head. It didn't make any sense, but they needed to get back to town and make sure the people were safe.

As they ran back, Akari noticed Takeo kept getting ahead of her, and he would have to slow down so she could catch up. Then she remembered that, as a fae, he had supernatural speed.

"Hey," Akari finally called out. "You can go on ahead, see what is happening. I will catch up."

"If you give me your hand," Takeo said with a smirk. "I can help you run faster."

"Really?" Akari asked. Takeo nodded. She reached out and took his hand, instantly feeling a boost of speed. Her feet didn't seem to be moving any faster, but the wind at her face and the speed at which they were passing things along the road told her they were moving faster than normal. It was an exhilarating feeling, like flying.

The feeling quickly dissipated, though, when they got close enough to town and they could hear the screams.

"My gods," Akari gasped when they arrived. There was smoke rising from burning buildings. There were several bodies on the ground, drained of their life force. People were running from demons of all sorts—oni, ōkami, bakeneko, yurei, and much more.

Akari drew her sword and rushed toward the nearest demon, an oni with a white face and horns that had been chasing a young woman. The creature roared at her, trying to intimidate, but Akari could not be cowed. She easily decapitated the monster with one swipe.

"Thank you," the woman said as she ran toward Akari.

"What happened?" Akari asked.

"I don't know," the woman said. "The ground shook, and then there was a sound like an explosion. Then the monsters flooded into town and..." The woman stopped speaking, and her face went blank.

Akari shook her arm. "And what?" she asked. Akari watched, horrified, as the woman's eyes turned black and her skin ashy. Dropping her eyes, she saw that the woman's feet were entangled in smoke. Akari stepped away and then hacked at the smoke with her sword, but it was too late. The woman crumpled to the ground like so many others who had been drained of their life force.

Takeo grabbed Akari's arm. "Come on," he said. "We need to

get out of here!" He pulled her and leaped onto the roof of a nearby building in one jump, dragging Akari along with him. From their new vantage point, they could see the full extent of the demon attack.

Sentient smoke was creeping through town, sucking the life force out of anyone it touched, human and fae alike. The monsters were running amuck, destroying homes and the marketplace. Some people were trying to fight back, but they were no match for the feral beasts.

"What can we do?" Akari asked. There were so many monsters, and the smoke that could drain them with a touch. She knew if they went back to the ground, they would be overwhelmed.

"We need to find the rest of the Sword Kissed," Takeo said.

"And Sera," Akari agreed. They rushed along the tops of the buildings, leaping from one to the next, using Takeo's speed to move them quickly. They were heading toward Sera's dojo. When they arrived, they did see several Sword Kissed fighting the demons, but not near as many as there should have been.

"Where is everyone?" Akari asked after she and Takeo jumped down next to the other Sword Kissed.

"I'm not sure," a Sword Kissed named Watase said as she impaled an ōkami. "But Sumida is there." She motioned to the soulless body of Sumida on the ground.

"They can drain Sword Kissed?" Akari asked, horrified, as she kicked a bakeneko.

"Nothing seems to be able to stop them," Watase said as she paused for a breath.

Akari turned to Takeo. He was wrestling with an onikuma. Even though he did not possess Sword Kissed abilities, he was at least able to injure or hold monsters back until a Sword Kissed was able to take the monster out.

"Every time we take one out," he said, panting, "three more seem to replace them!"

"Where is Sensei?" Akari asked of no one in particular as she hacked and slashed at any monster she could.

"They took her," another Sword Kissed named Kimura said. "She came out of the dojo, and a smoke demon enveloped her. It didn't drain her like the others, but it dragged her into the woods."

"And Kaya?" Akari asked of her best friend.

Kimura shook her head. "No idea."

"The woman said there was a large explosion," Takeo said with a grunt. "What was it? Where did it come from?"

"It seemed to come from west of town," Watase said. "But then the monsters arrived, so we did not have a chance to go see what it was."

"That could be where the monsters are coming from," Takeo said. "Akari, you go check it out. We will stay here and try to hold them back."

Akari hesitated. They were barely holding on as it was. She didn't want to leave her friends to defend themselves.

"*Go*," Watase yelled. "We need to stop them! They are going to overrun us at this pace."

Akari turned and ran toward the west. If she stopped to think about it, she wouldn't go. She had to fight her way through the monsters as she went, but she was quick and agile and able to make it outside of town.

She had just gotten beyond the town's border when she saw it —a large rift had opened in the ground. Monsters were pouring out of it. It reminded her of one of the paintings she and Takeo had seen in the temple. The world was tearing itself apart. But why? Why now after so many centuries?

More importantly, how could she stop this rift before it grew even bigger?

She fought her way to the rift and called down into it, "Chiyoko, I am here! Teach me to help you!"

Akari saw something coming up the rift toward her. She

strained to see what it was in the darkness. She only realized too late it was the largest oni she had ever seen.

The beast roared as it jumped out of the rift, knocking her backward and pinning her to the ground. She dropped her sword just out of reach. The beast opened its mouth and growled fiercely, dripping its pungent drool on her face.

Akari growled back and tried to push the beast off her, but it was too heavy.

They were at an impasse. It couldn't kill her, but she couldn't fight back. She looked around, trying to figure out a new plan, but then she felt her back get wet. Then rain began to fall, lightly at first, but soon it was pouring. She heard a rumbling and lifted her gaze just as a torrent of water started rushing down the hill toward her. It knocked the beast off her and back into the rift. After she grabbed her sword, she plunged it into the ground. She held on tight to keep from being washed away. Some of the monsters with large claws had also managed to hold on and keep from being swept away.

"Ayiii-ya!" several small voices yelled. The kappa they had met in the forest were running toward the monsters, poking them with their sticks, forcing them to let go and be washed away.

Soon, the flash flood had washed all the creatures away and was running toward town. She hoped the waters would clean away the monsters there as well. She looked in the direction from which the flood had come and saw Ameonna drifting toward her.

"Ameonna," Akari yelled. She stood up and ran toward her. "You saved me! Thank you! But how did you know?"

"We hill folk are connected to the earth," she said. "I heard you call to Chiyoko." She then waved someone else over.

A small green creature with clothes made of leaves drifted down on vines of ivy. She was a kodama, a tree spirit. The kodama went over to the rift, and then laid her hands on the ground. Instantly, plants, flowers, tree roots, and vines grew together to stitch the rift closed.

"This will not hold the rift closed for long," the kodama said in her small lilting voice. "But it is the best I can do for now."

"We seem to be growing weaker as Chiyoko grows more ill," Ameonna said sadly. "But we will defend the earth for as long as we can."

"That is all any of us can do," Akari said. "This is a great help. It will at least buy us time while we figure out what to do next."

Akari thanked all the hill creatures before hurrying back to Takeo and her fellow Sword Kissed. Without thinking, she ran up and hugged Takeo when she saw he was safe, but then she quickly pulled away.

"What happened?" Takeo asked. "It was as though a river came out of nowhere and swept the monsters away."

Akari nodded. "That's exactly what happened. The hill sprites, they came to help. Ameonna washed them away while a kodama sealed the rift, for now anyway."

"What should we do?" Kimura asked. "They will come back, and we are still missing several Sword Kissed."

"We need to group," Akari said. "We need to find the rest of the team and Sera. We have to work together. We aren't strong enough alone to defeat this."

"I wouldn't plan on finding Sera anytime soon," Kimura said. "There is no telling where that smoke monster took her."

"That is a good point," Takeo said. "What about Kaya?"

"If I can't talk to Sera," Akari said, "then I should find Yoshimi. She still might know something that can help us interpret what we learned at the temple."

Takeo nodded. "Okay, you find Yoshimi. We will look for the rest of the Sword Kissed."

Akari nodded and headed toward her house. As she went through town, she was distraught at the level of damage she saw. There were so many people who were dead and injured. And while the flood did wash away the monsters, it had swept away innocent people and destroyed more homes as well. But she could not stop to help the people now. She needed to stop the threat, then they could rebuild.

When she arrived at her house, though, she realized she had not been spared the destruction.

The roof of her house had caved in.

14

"Yoshimi!" Akari called as she climbed the steps to her house. "Are you here?" She forced the door open. Nearly everything in the house had been destroyed, the furniture, the walls, the decorations. The roof was all over the floor, and she could see the clear blue sky above. She had a feeling the flood did not do this. There was no water anywhere. She only hoped Yoshimi and Elwin had not been home when the house was attacked.

She was about to leave the house when she heard a creak from a back room.

"Yoshimi?" She stumbled over piles of roof tiles scrambling to get to the noise. "I'm here," she yelled. As she got to the back of the house, there was still a wall and door intact that led to the bathroom. She tried to open the door, but it was stuck. "Hello? Yoshimi?"

"Sakura...sakura..." a low voice said with almost a laugh, as though taunting her.

Akari felt her anger rise. She drew her sword, and then used all her strength to kick down the door.

She saw Endo standing there, but she was no longer herself. She was three times her normal size and half smoke demon. She was holding Yoshimi in one large clawed hand. Yoshimi was unconscious. The outside wall to the bathroom was gone.

"Endo," Akari growled as she lit her sword. "Let my sister go."

Endo laughed. "Give me the map," she said. "And I will let her go."

Akari didn't even hesitate. She would give anything to protect her sister. She reached into her pocket, but the map was gone.

"I...I don't know where it is," she said. "But we didn't find anything there anyway. Just an old temple ruin."

Endo's face twisted in a grimace, and she moved her hand toward Yoshimi.

"Sakura," Akari yelled. "Sakura! Why do you keep taunting me? Who are you? Who am I to you? Are you Chiyoko?"

Endo's face writhed, as if she were fighting something, and then it disappeared in the smoke. Another face appeared, one that looked like the face of the statue in the temple. "We are all Chiyoko," the face said.

"I know you are sick," Akari said. "Tell me how to help you."

"There is great evil in the world," Chiyoko said. "My mother buried us in the earth to save the world. But it was too late. There was a darkness even deeper in the earth, older than time itself. I spent centuries trying to hold it back..." Her face grimaced in pain, and she started to fade. "I cannot...cannot..."

Her face vanished, and Endo's reappeared.

"Stay back, Akari," Endo said. "Or I'll devour your sister's soul right now! I need them. I need the energy to grow. I won't hesitate to take as many as I need to get back to my full strength!"

Akari took a step back and lowered her sword. "Whatever you want, I'll do," Akari said. "Just don't hurt her."

"The end has come," Endo said. "Do not interfere or try to stop us again. Stay away for two more days, and I will give you back your sister."

"What happens in two days?" Akari asked.

"The end of the world," Endo said.

With that, she flew from the room and into the woods, clutching Yoshimi in her smoky grasp.

Akari ran to edge of the house. "Yoshimi," she yelled into the darkening sky. She thought she heard whimpering, but it might have just been her imagination. She stood there for a moment, afraid to look away. She might never see her sister again. She finally took a step back, crunching broken bathroom tiles under her feet.

Two days. The end of the world. What was going to happen in two days? Whatever it was, could she really let it happen? She wanted to save her sister, but if she let the earth be destroyed, what would her sister be coming back to? Could she really live with herself if she let the world end in the hopes of saving one person? Would Yoshimi want her to? Could Yoshimi ever forgive her?

No. Yoshimi was far too selfless for that. Yoshimi would want her to stop whatever evil Chiyoko had been unable to stop.

But what could Akari do?

She made her way back to the front of her house, carefully stepping over the remnants of her life. Her mother's favorite serving dish. Her father's ink stone. A framed family photo. She picked it up and held it to her chest.

As she was exiting the house, Takeo ran up.

"Akari," he called.

She fell into his arms. "Yoshimi," she cried. "Endo took her!"

"Endo?" he asked as he held her tight. "She came back?"

"It looked as though she had completely merged with the demon that had inhabited her," Akari said. "She was half Endo and half smoke."

"I fear we may not be able to save her," he said.

"I know," Akari said. She slightly pulled away, still gripping the photo in her hand. "But she took Yoshimi. We have to find her."

"Why did she take her?" he asked. He stroked her cheek and wiped away her tears. "Did she say anything?"

"She told me to stop interfering," Akari said. "To let the evil do what it wanted for two more days and she would return Yoshimi."

"What happens in two days?" Takeo asked.

"The end of the world," Akari said.

Takeo sighed and held her tight. "That doesn't sound good."

"She still wanted the map," Akari said. "She must think there is something of value on the mountain."

"She probably just thinks we are hiding something," Takeo said. "If she doesn't know what is there, the curiosity must be killing her."

"She always wanted whatever I had," Akari said with a sad chuckle. "Did you find Sera?" she asked, suddenly remembering why Takeo had stayed behind.

"No," he said, shaking his head. "Nor did I find Kaya."

Akari shook her head before turning back to face the shell of her house. "I feel so useless, so helpless. We have been tracking this thing for days, but we've learned nothing! Things have gone from bad to worse. Now my sister is gone, my mentor is lost, and my best friend is probably dead!" She rubbed her arms as the tears threatened to come again.

Takeo wrapped his arms around her. "Not all is lost," he said. "You have your strength. You still have some fellow Sword Kissed left. And..." He paused.

Akari turned. "And...?" she asked.

"And you have me," he said.

Akari leaned in and kissed him. It might not have been the smartest thing she could do in that moment, but she needed the contact, the reassurance, the warmth of his touch.

She felt him start to pull away, as if he too was not certain they should be doing this, but she stepped forward, telling him with her body that she wanted this, just for a moment.

He held her close, running his fingers through her hair. She opened her mouth and sucked on his lower lip. He tasted good. She could imagine this could go much further than one kiss. Maybe after all this was over...

She finally pulled back. "Sorry," she mumbled. "I shouldn't have...We need to focus on Chiyoko and stopping the demons."

"Don't apologize," he said. "Maybe when this is over..."

"*If* it's ever over," she interjected. "We have no way to stop it. We don't even really know what we are dealing with. For a moment, Chiyoko took over Endo's body. She said there was a...a darkness older and more powerful than her taking over the world. If she can't contain it, what chance do we have?"

"We have to believe there is a chance," Takeo said. "Otherwise, why keep going?"

She took a deep breath and nodded uneasily. He was right. They had to keep going, keep fighting. It would at least give them something to do while they waited for the end of the world.

"Elwin," Takeo gasped as he looked up at the house, as though seeing the destruction for the first time. "Where is Elwin?"

"I don't know," Akari said. "I didn't see him inside."

Takeo held his hands up and closed his eyes, as if he were sensing something. "I can feel him," Takeo said. "He must be hiding." He leaped up the stairs and went through where the door used to be. "Elwin?" he called.

Akari followed, feeling a little guilty she had completely forgotten about the boy.

Takeo went into the guest room where Elwin had been sleeping. "Elwin?" he asked again.

"Here," a small voice replied. The futon mattress was leaning up against the wall and was covered with debris. The mattress moved a little bit. Takeo pulled the mattress down, and there was Elwin, completely unharmed.

Akari could almost feel Takeo's relief wash over him as he ran to the boy and took him in his arms.

"Elwin-chan! You did a great job hiding," Takeo said.

"The house started to shake," Elwin said with a whimper. "Yoshimi-san told me to hide. I didn't want to leave her, but I was so scared. Is she okay?"

"Yoshimi will be fine," Takeo said to comfort the boy, even though he had no way to know if it was true or not. He picked up Elwin and turned to Akari. "We need to find someone else to care for him until this is over."

Akari nodded. She started to leave the house, but she stopped and placed the photo on what used to be the family altar. She kowtowed three times, asking for the blessings of her ancestors, something she hadn't done in ages.

Takeo came up behind her. "Who...who is in the picture?" he asked.

Akari pointed to the people in the photo. "My father, Yoshimi, me, my mother, and my grandmother. Mother's mother. She lived with us toward the end."

"You look like your mother," he said.

She shrugged. "I guess. I always thought Yoshimi looked like her more than me."

"Are you joking?" he asked, but when he saw she was serious, the smile ran from his face. "Well, we can debate that later, I guess. Let's go."

He led the way out of the house and toward the village of Kuji.

*I*t was dark by the time they arrived. The village was quiet and seemed empty. Even at night, there should have been people out and about, taking care of their homes and livestock, enjoying an after-dinner walk, or visiting neighbors, but there was hardly anyone to be seen.

Galen, the son of the village elder who had disappeared, came out to greet them.

"I don't suppose you have returned with good news?" he asked.

Akari shook her head, disappointed with herself. "Quite the opposite, I'm afraid. One of the demons took Yoshimi and destroyed our home."

"They took Yoshimi-chan? No!"

Akari couldn't hide the shock on her face that the man used the affectionate honorific of "chan." Maybe Yoshimi *was* interested in a fae man...

Galen cleared his throat. "I mean, I am sorry to hear about Yoshimi-san's disappearance. She is much loved here."

"I am going to do whatever it takes to get her back," Akari said.

"Whatever you need of us, just ask," Galen replied. "I heard about the demon attack on the town. Things are getting worse by the minute."

By this point, an exhausted Elwin had fallen asleep in Takeo's arms. "We have not given up," he said. "We are going to try and find Yoshimi and stop the growing evil. But we need someone to take care of the boy."

The man nodded, waving the lilac maid forward. She came out of the hut and took Elwin back inside with her.

"We will care for him as one of our own," the man said with a bow toward Takeo.

"Where is everyone?" Akari asked as she rubbed her arms. It appears a chill had settled over the village as well.

The man seemed to hesitate for a moment. "They have...gone elsewhere. They think they will be safer far from this place."

"If we don't stop whatever is happening, they won't be safe anywhere," Akari lamented. She surveyed the village and then felt a little dizzy, a bit confused. She was certain a house they had passed on the way into town was now gone. "What...what is happening?" she asked, gripping Takeo's arm. "The town...it seems smaller somehow."

The man grimaced and shot Takeo a look.

"While searching for answers," Takeo explained, "we pierced a veil, the one on the mountain. The veil you are using to obfuscate your village must not be very strong if Akari can sense it."

"The village is veiled?" Akari asked.

Takeo nodded. He held his hand over Akari's eyes for a moment and then removed it.

Akari gasped. The village was at least twice the size she thought it was, and it was full of people.

"So, your people aren't going anywhere," Akari said. "You are just trying to hide in plain sight."

"We have to do something to protect ourselves," Galen said.

"But...Kuji has never been this big," Akari said. "You've been veiling at least half the village for...for how long?"

"For its entire existence," he said.

"Remember when I told you the fae were veiling more than you could have imagined?" Takeo asked. Akari nodded. "They are hiding entire fae cities."

"My gods," Akari said. "If the humans knew about this..."

"They would think the fae were a threat to them, a danger," he said. "But the whole reason they hide is because they have been treated so badly by humans in the first place. They don't feel safe living openly."

Akari gawked at the village—the town—again. It was even

larger than Nasu. She shook her head, wondering just how much about this world she didn't know. She felt like she knew nothing about her past—her own or the history of Chiyoko Hollow. And she had been just as blind to the world she was living in now. To make matters worse, the world she was only just now discovering was about to change. It could all end in two days. Or if they somehow succeeded and destroyed the evil, the world would not be the same one she thought she knew before. And things needed to change. The fae should not live in such fear, and the humans could not continue oppressing the fae.

Akari was not sure she was ready for what was to come.

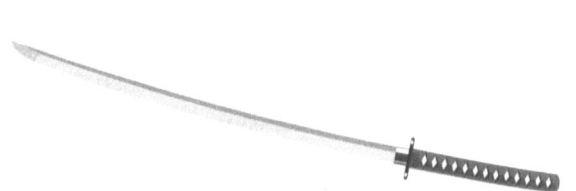

15

"So even though it could cost my sister her life," Akari said as they left Kuji, "we have decided to keep fighting."

Takeo nodded. "We can never give up."

"But what should we do? How should we fight?" she asked. "Sera is gone, as is Yoshimi. I was hoping they had some answers. I don't even have the map anymore."

"Oh," Takeo said, looking sheepish as he reached into his pocket and handed the map to her. "I have it."

"Why do *you* have it?" she asked, snatching it back.

"I...I took it from you," he admitted. "I wasn't sure I could trust you with it when I began suspecting it was more than just pointing the way through the veil for you."

"What do you mean?" she asked, irritated. After all they had been through together, he still didn't trust her?

"The reason the monsters want it is because it is a veil key," he said. "The veil over the mountain is so powerful that even fae cannot see through it without a key. I think it is why you were able to sense the veil in Kuji. The key's magic was still active on you long after you had last touched it."

"So the monsters know the veil is there, but they can't see through it without this?" Akari asked. Takeo nodded. "Which makes me wonder more about Sera. Why would she have something so powerful?"

"Let's go back to her dojo," he said. "Maybe we will find answers there."

hen they arrived back at the dojo, it had mostly been destroyed. Akari stepped gingerly through the rubble, afraid she might step on something precious. She noticed Takeo was holding his hands up and his eyes were closed. She knew by now he was trying to sense fae energy.

"There is...a lot of fae energy here," he said, not opening his eyes.

"Is it Sera?" Akari asked. "Is she fae?"

"I can't tell without her here," he said. "But there was a veil here. She—or someone—was using fae energy to mask something that was here. But it's gone now."

"The veil or what the veil was hiding?" Akari asked.

"Both," Takeo said.

"Damn," Akari cursed under her breath as she kicked at a bit of rubble. "Another dead end..."

A gentle breeze blew, and a few cherry blossoms tumbled across the destroyed building. Akari kneeled and picked one up.

"Are you a human or are you a fairy?" she mumbled. Takeo was half fae. Akari probably had some fae ancestry. Sera was almost certainly a full fae. Chiyoko Hollow was named after a fae goddess. She wondered just how much of the world was fae. For so long, humans had thought they were the dominant species. That their sheer numbers gave them authority over the rest of the creatures in the world. What was going to happen if the veils came down and the humans realized that not only did the fae outnumber them, but many of them probably had fae blood?

"Do you remember in the painting in the temple?" Akari said. "There was one where humans and fae were living side by side in both worlds. It stands to reason they were intermarrying."

"Sure," Takeo said. "There is no biological reason they wouldn't. I'm living proof of that."

"What if..."

"Akari-chan," Kaya called.

Akari turned and was shocked to see her friend standing there. She ran up to her and embraced her tightly.

"Kaya-chan," she said, looking at her friend's face. "I'm so glad to see you! Where have you been?"

"I was out patrolling when the monsters attacked," she said. "I got separated from the others."

"I have so much to tell you," Akari said.

"What did you find on the mountain?' Kaya asked.

"Yes," Akari said. "That's part of it. I will tell you. But Yoshimi is missing. I really need your help..."

"So what was it?" Kaya asked. "On the mountain?"

Akari paused. She was going to get to that, but Yoshimi being missing was a little more important. "There was just a temple," Akari said. "Nothing else."

"Are you sure?" Kaya asked. "You brought nothing back? Learned nothing that could stop the demons?"

"No," Akari said, and she stared deeply in Kaya's eyes. There was a hardness there, a coldness. And Kaya was neither hard nor cruel. Akari gripped Kaya's arm. "Who are you?" she asked. "Are you Chiyoko? The demon who inhabited Endo? Who?"

Kaya laughed, pushing Akari away with a force that shocked her and caught her off guard. Akari flew backward and landed hard on the ground.

"Remember your promise," Kaya said with a deep, dark voice that was not her own. "For two days, you will not interfere..." She opened her mouth. Smoke poured out and dissipated into the air. Kaya then collapsed to the ground.

Akari ran to her side. "Kaya," she cried, shaking her awake.

"Wha...what happened?" Kaya asked in her own voice as her eyes fluttered open.

"Are you all right?" Akari asked.

Kaya sat up and rubbed her head. "I don't know," she said. "I feel nauseous."

"I can imagine being inhabited by a demon would do that to a person," Takeo said.

"Inhabited?" Kaya asked. "I don't remember. I just felt the rumbling, heard the explosion. I saw the demons coming toward me. I drew my sword and then...nothing."

"One of the demons must have possessed you early on," Akari said. "The battle was fierce. Some of the Sword Kissed and townspeople were killed. Much of the town destroyed."

"Oh my gods," Kaya said. She stood up uneasily. Akari held her arm to steady her. "We have to stop them."

"I have stopped them for now," Akari said. "A hill spirit washed them away. But they will be back. One of them told me the end of the world is coming in two days."

"What can we do?" she asked. "We need to ask Sera for guidance."

"We can't," Akari said. "Sera is gone. She was taken. As was Yoshimi."

"Oh no," Kaya exclaimed, taking Akari in her arms and giving her a tight hug. "I'm so sorry. But she was taken, not killed. So there is still hope."

Akari hugged her friend back and released her. "Yes, we need to keep fighting."

"So, what should we do?" Kaya asked. "What have you learned so far?"

Akari took a deep breath. She tried to recount everything she knew, everything that had happened. "Chiyoko was buried to try and save the world, to protect it from evil forces. But she has been overrun, and she's now the evil infecting the world and the creatures in it. We have to stop her."

"But you are sure you learned nothing in the temple that can help?" Kaya asked.

"I'm sure," Akari replied, exasperated. "Why does everyone keep asking that? It was just old history."

Takeo gasped. "Everyone does keep asking that. Akari, what if we did miss something?"

"I thought the demons just wanted to know what was on the mountain because they didn't know what was there," Akari said.

"But what if we were wrong?" he asked. "What if Sera didn't just send us there as a training mission? What if we were supposed to find something?"

"The nightblooms!" Akari said. "We never found the cave under the temple. We got so wrapped up in the paintings at the ruins, I completely forgot to find the caves and the nightblooms."

"Maybe there is something in the caves," he said. "The answer to defeating Chiyoko."

"Come on," Akari said taking his hand. "We need to get back up there fast!"

16

*T*akeo held Akari's hand, and they ascended the mountain at record speed. When they arrived at the old temple, things were not as they had left it.

"It's so dark," Akari said. It should only have been mid-day, but there were clouds and smoke and ash blocking the sun, creating a choking haze.

Takeo kneeled and placed a hand to the earth. "Do you feel that rumbling?"

Akari nodded. There was a constant low shaking, as if the earth was grumbling.

"It feels like the mountain is about to blow," she said, and they shot each other worried looks.

At one time, Chiyoko had been plagued by earthquakes, volcanoes, and tsunamis. But since the Great Divide, the earth had been calm. There had not been a significant natural disaster in the history of Chiyoko. But everyone feared the day they might return.

"We need to find the cave," Takeo said.

Akari pulled out the map. "Here is the temple," she said,

pointing to it. The map showed a trail behind the temple leading down the backside of the mountain. "The cave must be here."

They ran around the temple, finding an extremely overgrown trail. Akari drew her sword and hacked their way through the underbrush.

"There it is," Takeo said, nearly pushing Akari over to get to the cave in his excitement.

Akari's excitement was a bit more subdued. When they discovered the temple, her entire heritage, her family history, hell the history of the world, all of it changed. She wasn't sure she was looking forward to whatever they were going to find.

Takeo stopped before entering the cave. He must have seen the apprehension on her face because he gave her a reassuring smile and held out his hand.

"Come on," he said. "We will do this together."

Akari took his hand, and they entered the cave. When they stepped inside, Akari gasped.

It was beautiful.

The cave was brighter than the sky outside. There were countless nightblooms, their petals spread and emitting soft yellow and purple light. The lichen growing on the stalactites and walls also glowed.

"Sera," Akari called. On the floor of the cave in the middle of the room, Sera was unconscious. Even though her face was turned away, Akari would know Sera anywhere. She ran to Sera's side. But when she turned Sera's face to her, she did not see a face she recognized.

Sera was fae.

Her skin was lilac colored, and she had grey-to-black mottling around her hairline. Her ears were pointed, and she had small horns at her temples.

Akari couldn't help but gasp. She was relieved to have found her here, but she also felt betrayed. Lied to. Part of her was angry. Why had so much been kept from her?

"Sera," Akari yelled, and she shook Sera's shoulders. "Wake up, damn it!" She noticed the front of Sera's robe was green with fae blood. She opened the robe a bit, but she didn't find any injuries.

Takeo placed a hand on Akari's arm. She looked up at him, and he appeared blurry through the tears she would not allow to fall. He reached down and placed two fingers on Sera's neck.

"She is alive," he said. "But weak."

"What is she doing here?" Akari asked. "How did she get here?"

Takeo's eyes widened and he quickly stood, facing the cave's entrance.

"What is it?" Akari asked.

"Nothing," he said. "Just standing guard. But you are right. She was abducted by one of the smoke monsters. If she is here, they might not be far behind."

"She waits there also..." Akari mumbled. "Is Sera the 'she' from the haiku?"

Takeo shrugged. "I wouldn't think so. The poem is old. Older than Sera, by the look of her true form."

Akari laid Sera back down and examined the cave. "Then what were we supposed to find here?"

"You look around," Takeo said as he walked toward the cave opening. "I'll keep an eye on the entrance."

Akari nodded and walked around the cave. There was a small creek running through it, and water from the ceiling made dripping noises into it. She ran her hands over some of the night-bloom flowers, and their iridescent pollen stuck to her fingers.

The cave seemed to go on and on with no end in sight. She squinted in the darkness, wondering how far she should continue, and saw something strange on a far wall.

In glowing ink, probably made from the petals of the night-bloom flowers, was one more painting similar to the ones in the temple.

In this painting, there was a large dark beast with the face of Chiyoko terrorizing the world. And facing the beast was a woman with a glowing sword.

Akari's heart raced.

She already knew what she was looking at, but she held her breath as she went in for a closer look.

The woman in the painting was Akari.

Akari was going to have to face Chiyoko. She searched the room for more paintings. She went deeper into the cave. There were fewer flowers the further she went, the cave growing darker and darker. But there were no more paintings.

She had to know if she would win.

How could the painter know so much? Paint the battle that was to come and not know what would happen? How could this unknown artist send Akari to fight, to stop the end of the world without hope?

And more importantly—why Akari?

"Akari?" Takeo yelled into the cave. "Where are you? Come back!"

Akari headed toward his voice and ran into his arms. "Did you see it?" she cried. "Did you see what will happen?"

He stroked her hair and held her tight. "I saw it."

"How can I do this? How can I fight Chiyoko?"

"Because it is your destiny," he said. "This is your purpose."

Akari stood back and shook her head. "But I'm no one. I'm Sword Kissed, yes, but so is Kaya. Why not her? So is Endo, and she let herself be possessed by the darkness. So was Sumida, and she's dead! If they couldn't stand against the darkness that has infected the world, how can I?"

Takeo took Akari's forearms in his hands, giving her a small shake. "Open your eyes, Akari! Can't you see it?"

She only felt confusion. "See what?"

He dragged her over to the painting, and then forced her to

look at it. "I know you can see through the veil. But you are fighting it. Stop fighting, Akari. Just let go. Open your eyes!"

And then Akari saw the painting as if for the first time.

Chiyoko's face was one she knew well. It was the face of her mother. The face of her grandmother.

It was her own face.

She had always known she resembled her mother. She just said Yoshimi looked like their mother to make her feel better. She knew Yoshimi was jealous Akari was Sword Kissed. But something must have been preventing her—and everyone else—from realizing their faces were identical.

The face that had been passed down from generation to generation, just like the sakura song.

"I'm not just Sword Kissed," Akari said as the realization dawned on her. "I'm a direct descendant of Chiyoko herself."

She felt Takeo's grip on her arms loosen.

"How long have you known?" she asked him.

"When we went to the ruins of your house," he said. "You picked up the picture of you, your mother, and grandmother. I saw it then. But you didn't. Or at least, you didn't say anything. You were so overwhelmed by the loss of Yoshimi, I didn't want to question you then. But I knew."

"I didn't want to see," Akari said. "It was just...too much. I couldn't handle more revelations."

"You are stronger than you give yourself credit for," Takeo said, stroking her face. "You will save us all."

Akari stepped back and shook her head. "The painting shows me confronting her. It doesn't show me winning."

"You will," Takeo said with a confidence Akari wished she had. "You have me. You have Kaya. If she wakes up, you will have Sera. You are not alone like the painting shows."

They then both heard a groan from the front of the cave.

"Sera," Akari said, and they ran to her side.

Sera was stirring. She placed her hand to her head.

"Sensei." Akari took Sera in her arms. "You are alive!"

"Barely, Akari-chan," she said with a small smile. She opened her eyes. Reaching out, she touched Akari's cheek. "You can see...finally..."

Akari nodded. "Yes. Takeo forced me to."

"I knew he would be a good partner," Sera said weakly.

"How did you get here?" Akari asked, holding Sera tightly to keep her warm.

"I fought the demon that took me, but I was injured," she explained.

Takeo grabbed a cup from his pack. He went to the small stream to get some water, which he brought back to Sera. She drank it eagerly.

"Thank you, Torgwyn-san," Sera said. "I used the last of my strength, of my fae magic, to transport myself here. This cave is said to have healing abilities."

"Your injuries appear to have healed," Akari confirmed. "But it will take a while for you to regain your strength."

"And for your magic to recharge," Takeo said.

Sera nodded and forced herself to sit. Akari still helped keep her steady.

"I'm glad you are safe, Sensei," Akari said. "But you and I need to have a long talk."

Sera gave a small chuckle, but then winced in pain. "Eventually," she said. "But there is no time. We must..."

They all froze as they felt the earth shake violently. Akari and Sera held each other as Takeo made his way to the cave entrance. Akari then saw him take a step back.

Endo, almost completely a demonic creature of smoke except for her face, entered the cave.

"Thank you for leading me here," Endo said. "I knew it would only be a matter of time."

Takeo drew his daggers and leaped at Endo, but she batted

him away as though he were merely a fly. He smashed into the cave wall, slumping unconscious to the floor.

Akari gritted her teeth and got to her feet. She drew her katana, and she lit it with her palm.

"This ends now, Endo," she yelled.

Endo laughed. "For you it does."

Akari ran at Endo and slashed at the smoke, but nothing happened. She stepped out of the way as Endo took a swipe at her.

Endo laughed again. "Your pitiful Sword Kissed powers are nothing. I have grown too powerful!"

Akari felt her heart race. She shot a look at Sera. Sera had dragged herself to a stalagmite and was leaning up against it. She was panting hard, obviously drained from the exertion.

What was she supposed to do? All she had were her Sword Kissed powers. If that was not enough to defeat Endo, then what else did she have? Takeo was out cold. Sera was depleted.

They were doomed.

17

*S*akari...sakura...

    Akari wasn't sure how much stock she put into prophecies. She'd never given much thought to it before. If she believed the painting on the wall, then she wasn't going to die here. Not at the hands of Endo. She was destined to face Chiyoko.

Sakura...

Endo continued laughing, swiping only half-heartedly at Akari. She knew she had the advantage. She only had to tire Akari out, then she could take her down.

But there was someone else here. Akari could hear...something. Someone singing the sakura song.

Akari continued to hold her sword aloft and slashed at Endo whenever she got too close, even if it did no good.

"Who are you?" Akari asked Endo. "Why are you singing that song?"

"I'm not singing," Endo growled as she lunged forward. "I'm relishing in your death!"

"Endo," Sera called weakly. "What happened? How could you

let this thing take you? You are Sword Kissed. The light of Chiyoko shines in you!"

"Shut up," Endo yelled, turning her attention to Sera. "You'll get your turn. But not before you get to watch your precious star student go first!"

"This is not you, Endo-chan," Sera said as she struggled to sit up. "You are better than this."

"How would you know? How dare you call me chan," Endo shrieked, her smoke coils slowly encircling Sera.

"Don't touch her," Akari yelled, running forward. But Endo slapped her away with a smoke trail. Akari rolled when she hit the ground, protecting her head to keep from being knocked unconscious.

"You only had eyes for Akari," Endo continued. "You never saw I was faster. Stronger. Smarter!"

Sera shook her head. "Your ego was always your downfall," she said. "You could never see the bigger picture."

Endo shrieked, and Akari saw Sera was gripping one of Endo's smoke trails, squeezing it like a snake and sending an electric shock through it. The smoke demon dissipated, and Endo's body appeared and slumped to the ground.

Akari ran to Sera, who was so weak she could barely keep her eyes open.

"Sensei," Akari cried. "Why did you do that? You are too weak. I will protect you."

"I know you will, Akari-chan," she said. Her eyes fluttered closed. "I know..."

Her body went completely limp. Akari had no idea if she were alive or dead, but she didn't have time to waste. Endo was already stirring. But so was Takeo. She went to Takeo's side and helped him up.

"What happened?" he asked as he stood.

"Sera shocked Endo, but only for a moment. We need to get out of here!"

He shook his head. "We will never outrun her. We have to fight. *You* have to fight."

"But...how?" Akari asked. "I...I..."

"Akari..." Endo moaned as she slowly awoke and smoke started to gather around her.

"I don't know what to do," Akari yelled.

Sakura...sakura...

A gentle breeze blew. Akari saw cherry blossoms blow across the cave floor and toward the painting. Akari ran to it. Takeo was right behind her.

> *"Where the nightbloom grow*
> *Is where my heart will find you*
> *She waits there also."*

Akari recited the haiku hurriedly. "There must be something here. Something in the painting. Something I'm missing. Something she is trying to tell me..."

She ran her hands over it, as if searching for a switch. Something to trigger a memory or realization.

"Akari..." Endo sat up, and the smoke coiled more thickly around her.

"Shit," Akari cursed. She drew her sword. "We are out of..." Her sword caught her attention. Then she looked back at the painting. She knew what she had to do.

"Stay here," she told Takeo. "Do your best to hold her off!"

He nodded and drew his bow.

Akari ran toward the cave opening, past Endo. Endo reached for her, but she was still weak and moved slowly. Takeo shot an arrow through Endo's smoky tentacle, and she roared in pain. As Akari flew out of the cave and up the trail, she glanced back and saw Endo turning her attention to Takeo. She hoped he would survive long enough...just a minute...

Akari ran to the temple and threw open the door. Everything

was the same as she had left it, except now Chiyoko's face and hers were the same. It was chilling, but Akari had to hurry. She ran to the statue, and then pulled the katana from Chiyoko's hand free. As Akari gripped the hilt, she felt a surge of power course through her and the katana glowed bright pink, like the center of a cherry blossom. She didn't even need to slice her hand and use her blood to ignite it. She and the katana were one.

Chiyoko must have known that this would happen, Akari thought. That she couldn't hold back the evil forever. That she might end up becoming the evil she had sacrificed herself to stop. She had left everything in place to fight back when the evil rose again. Akari just had to put the pieces together. The Sword Kissed. The paintings in the temple. The cave. The katana.

Akari ran back down the hill. When she arrived back at the cave, she saw Endo had regained her strength. She had Takeo in her grip, seeming as if she were about to tear him apart.

"Endo," Akari called, and Endo smiled. "I'm ready for you now."

Endo laughed. "I've been ready for you for a long time." She dropped Takeo, and he landed with a grunt. She then lunged toward Akari.

Akari's forehead dripped with sweat, and her heart beat wildly. But she licked her lip and dug her foot into the ground to gain traction. She yelled as she ran straight at Endo, the smoke demon.

Endo let out a horrifying scream as Akari's sword sliced through her. Akari had had nearly rent Endo in half. Endo was shrieking and panicking. She grasped at her smoke tendrils as they started to melt, and her along with it.

"No! No," she cried. "This can't be happening! Chiyoko, you promised me! Ahh!"

Like the enenra at Yahakami village, Endo melted into a pile of thick black tar. The floor of the cave absorbed her, and she was gone.

Akari panted for a moment, shocked she had taken Endo down with one strike, but she finally sheathed her sword. She walked over to where Endo had melted and kicked at the dirt, but there was nothing left.

"Akari-chan," Takeo said. She turned and saw him limping toward her.

"Takeo," she cried. She hurried over and let him lean on her. "Are you injured?"

He shook his head. "I just twisted my ankle, but I will be fine. Fae are fast healers. Your katana. It is from the statue."

"Yes," Akari said. "I thought it was just part of the sculpture at first, but then I noticed that in the painting, I was holding the same katana."

They made their way over to Sera, and Takeo checked her neck again. He nodded. "She is still alive. But we need to get her back to town. To Kuji. She needs a fae doctor."

Akari wasn't sure how they were going to do that. Sera was completely incapacitated, and Takeo was limping. She couldn't take either of them back to the village by herself.

"Yoshimi!" Akari gasped, just now remembering. "Endo had Yoshimi. Now that Endo is gone, where is she?"

"She's right here," a voice said.

Akari stood up and turned. She saw Chiyoko—who looked like herself but in different clothes, the more traditional robes— standing there with Yoshimi wrapped in smoke. Yoshimi was awake this time, her eyes wild with fear. But her mouth was covered with smoke, so she couldn't speak or scream.

"Let her go," Akari ordered. She went to grab her katana, but a smoke tendril shot out of Chiyoko's arm and pinned Akari against the wall.

"I warned you, Akari," Chiyoko said. "I warned you to stay away, or else Yoshimi would die."

"No," Akari said, struggling against the smoke tentacle. "Stop! You can stop this. You want me to stop this!"

"It's too late for that," Chiyoko said. "The world will end. And there is nothing you can do to stop it."

Chiyoko—along with her smoke and Yoshimi—vanished as quickly as they had arrived.

"No," Akari yelled as she ran to the cave entrance. "I'm coming for you," she screamed into the forest. "I am Sword Kissed Tanaka, and I will stop you!"

*a*kari helped Sera sip at the water from the cave's stream. As much as she wanted to chase after Chiyoko and take her down, she couldn't leave Sera and Takeo behind. After only a few minutes, Takeo's ankle was strong enough for him to walk on again.

"Hmm." He nodded with satisfaction as he tested putting his weight on his foot again. "Sera was right. There does seem to be something healing about this cave. I'm a fast healer, but this is impressive."

"You are sure you are strong enough?" Akari asked dubiously. She tied some branches and twigs together to fashion a makeshift stretcher, so they could carry Sera back down the mountain.

"I'll be fine," he said. "It's just a little sore."

They were working on laying Sera on the stretcher when they heard chittering from the cave entrance. They saw the kappa peeking in. Akari waved them over.

"It's safe, for now," she said. "Endo is gone."

"Friend sick?" one of them asked. They inched forward to investigate what was wrong with Sera.

Akari nodded and did her best to fight back tears. "Yes, my friend is sick. We have to get her to a doctor in Kuji village."

"Help! Help! Help," the kappa sang excitedly as they danced around, waving their sticks. They shouldered their way past Akari and Takeo. A dozen of them took hold of the stretcher, lifting it and carrying it to the cave entrance.

"Be careful," Akari cried, fussing around them like a mother hen. "She needs to be carried gently."

"Gentle! Gentle," they mimicked. Like a centipede, their little feet moved together, quickly and smoothly down the mountain. Akari was impressed by how cautious and efficient they were at getting Sera down the mountain. She was soon able to take a calming breath and a moment to think about what they needed to do next.

"I can't remember the last time I took a breath," she said to Takeo, who was walking with his head down, watching every step he took to make sure he didn't reinjure his ankle.

"You fought bravely," he said. "I know you are worried about Yoshimi, but with Chiyoko's katana, I think you have a real chance of beating her."

"We are running out of time," Akari said. "It might be too late. She is growing stronger. When she attacked me in the cave, she pinned me easily. The sword didn't matter. All she has to do is stay out of sight long enough to become too powerful for anyone to defeat."

"Then we need to find her first," Takeo said.

"How?" Akari asked.

"Let me talk to the elders at Kuji," he said. "They might know how to communicate with the fae in Ryu, or even in another Hollow."

"The radios," Akari said, excited. "You said there is a radio in

Ryu we could use to communicate with another Hollow and ask for help."

Takeo nodded. "Right, but Ryu is too far away. We could never get there in time to ask for help, much less get there and back."

Akari slipped her hand into Takeo's. "I want to thank you," she said softly. "I wouldn't have come this far without you."

"On my own, I could never hope to fight Chiyoko," he replied. "We are lucky to have found each other."

Akari chuckled and shook her head. "I can't believe I'm going to have to tell Sera-sensei she was right." She then felt a twinge of sadness as she watched Sera being carried down the hill. As much as she didn't look forward to having to humble herself before her teacher, she feared Sera never waking up at all more. Which reminded her of Yoshimi, and how she was still in Chiyoko's clutches. She felt her anxiety rise again, and she rubbed her chest.

Takeo squeezed her hand. "It will be all right," he said. "We will find a way to succeed."

Akari doubted he was right, but accepting defeat now would help no one. They had to keep fighting, even if it was a losing battle.

"We...have ways of communicating with the other Hollows," Galen said cautiously to Takeo. He gave Akari a side-eye. Akari crossed her arms and started to say something harsh about the fae communities' secrets putting them all in jeopardy, but Takeo cut her off, so she snapped her mouth shut.

"Have you heard anything about the others being under attack?" Takeo asked.

"Not directly," Galen said. He led them to a building—a proper sturdy building, not a hut. The village was not just larger than Akari and the other humans had been led to believe, but more advanced as well. "But the communications have been less frequent, and they've mentioned the other Hollows have been under distress."

"How have you been able to communicate?" Akari asked when they entered a room where several people were working.

"We have several radios that had been discarded by the human scientists as broken and worthless," Galen explained. "We were able to use fae magic to power them."

"Did you inform the scientists you were able to do this?" Akari asked. Galen and Takeo shot her a look. "I'm not trying to accuse you of anything," Akari tried to clarify. "But it could have been useful information. We should all be trying to work together."

"We did try," Galen said. "Without giving too much away, we tried explaining that certain crystals can be used as a power source. But they brushed us off, claiming we didn't know what we were talking about. So we took the dead radios and worked it out ourselves."

Akari nodded. She had no problem believing the humans would be too arrogant to try to use fae methods for powering the radios. And she knew the fae had reasons to be secretive and cautious when it came to working with humans. Still, the extent of what the fae had been hiding galled her, even though she knew it shouldn't. She still felt human, after all, and it would take a long time for her to fully sympathize with the fae.

"Malia," Galen called. A young greenish woman who was

wearing headphones turned around. She stood and gave Galen a bow.

"Yes, Naeran-san?" she asked.

"Have you been able to communicate with Katia Hollow?" he asked her.

"Yes, Naeran-san," she said. She sat back at her table before unplugging the headphones from the device in front of her. Akari had heard of the radios, but she had never seen one herself. It looked very complicated to use, but Malia was able to quickly turn the knobs and press the buttons to find what she was looking for.

"Katia Hollow," Malia said into a microphone. "This is Chiyoko Hollow, Kuji Village. Come in, Katia Hollow."

Akari knew Katia Hollow was to the northwest, what was formerly Russia.

"This is Katia Hollow. We read you, Chiyoko Hollow," a man's voice replied out of a speaker on the front of the radio. Akari couldn't help but gasp in excitement. She was hearing the voice of someone in a different Hollow. She never thought such a thing would be possible. He had a thick accent, which she found a little hard to understand, so she had to pay close attention to his words.

"That is amazing," Akari exclaimed. Takeo smiled and patted her on the back.

"You have much to learn of our world," he said.

"What would you like to ask them, Naeran-san?" Malia asked.

Galen motioned for Akari to speak into the microphone. Everything had happened so quickly, she hadn't given much thought to what she would ask them.

"Hello, Katia Hollow," Akari said. "My name is Akari Tanaka. Our hollow has been under attack by an evil force. It has been poisoning our world, creating evil monsters, and killing our people. Have you also been under attack?"

For a moment, Akari heard only static. She began to wonder

if she had done something wrong. But the voice on the other end finally replied.

"It's been bad here," he said. "Have you determined the source of the darkness?"

Akari chuckled. "If you haven't already discovered it for yourself, I'm not sure you'll believe me. But it is a fae goddess, one buried at the fracturing of the world and creation of the hollows."

The man on the other end laughed. "I hear you, Akari Tanaka. Who would have thought?"

"It has been a shocking couple of days," Akari said. "How are you coping? Have you found a way to fight back?"

"Not officially," the man said. "But there have been rumors of a woman, one who has found a weapon strong enough to fight back. I don't know if it's true, but I sure hope so."

She swung shocked eyes to Takeo, and he gave her a knowing nod. Akari turned back to the microphone. "I found a weapon, too. I'm just not sure if it will be strong enough...if I'm strong enough. I was hoping you had already defeated your goddess and could give me some tips on what I could do."

"I wish I could, Akari Tanaka," the man said. "But we are still fighting here. I don't know if the weapon this woman found will work or not. Last I heard, she was following some map to try to track the goddess down."

Akari's heart skipped, and she pulled out her own map. "Your woman has a map, too?" she asked. "I have one. It led me to the weapon."

"That's amazing," he said. "It must all be connected somehow. That's how our girl found her weapon, but she's still using it. Says it will lead her directly to the goddess."

Akari studied the map again. She turned it over and upside down. Flipping it over, she examined the back. She didn't see any other indications of anything else to look for.

"Mine just has a temple, where I found the weapon, and a

cave that had healing powers," Akari said into the microphone. "Do you know how she is using it to find the goddess?"

"Wish I did," he said. "I'm getting this information through the grapevine, if you know what I mean." Akari didn't, but she didn't interrupt. "Katia Hollow is huge, thousands of miles across. I don't know where the woman is or who she is or if any of this is true. Just rumors and hearsay. I wish I was more help."

Akari's heart dropped a little, but she still felt a twinge of hope that hadn't been there before. "No, you've told me a lot. At least there are enough similarities to know I'm on the right track. If that woman asks you for help, you do whatever she needs, okay?"

"Will do, Akari Tanaka," he said. "Good luck, Chiyoko Hollow."

Akari stood and backed away from the radio.

"That was incredible," Takeo said. "They have a map, a weapon, a woman putting it all together. Just like us! We are doing the right thing, Akari-chan."

Akari tried to absorb Takeo's excitement. But Katia Hollow had not defeated their goddess yet either. She wondered if the women in the other hollows were at the same point in their journeys as she was.

Were they all headed to victory at the same time, or death?

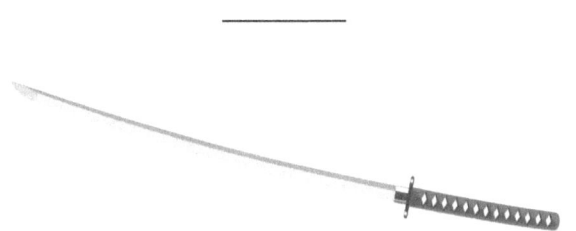

19

*A*kari went to the healer's hut, where Sera was being kept. She bowed to the healers as she entered, and they motioned that she was welcome to approach Sera. They were burning incense and had rubbed Sera's body with oils. They had placed some sort of poultice on her abdomen, where her original injury had been. The healers told Akari they had done all they could. That they had hopes she would recover, but it was all up to Sera now.

Akari stood by her teacher's side and took her hand. It felt cold and small. Not like the hand of the woman who had handed Akari her ass in the practice arena on countless occasions.

"Sera-sensei?" Akari whispered. Sera did not respond. "I don't know if you can hear me, but I hope you can." She sighed and pulled up a chair, so she could sit and speak closer to Sera's ear.

"I know I'm on the right path," Akari said. "We spoke to someone in another hollow. There was a woman there who also had a map and a weapon. And they knew about the buried goddesses. So far, I have been able to put the pieces together. I think Chiyoko knew this was going to happen, or she at least feared it would. But I am not sure what the next step is. I need to find Chiyoko before she grows too powerful. But I don't know where she is."

"Did you check the map?" Sera asked in a weak voice that was barely audible.

"Sensei?" Akari cried, lowering herself even closer to Sera's face. "You are awake! You are going to be fine!"

One of the healers rushed over and felt Sera's wrist. Then she placed her hand on Sera's chest. The healer nodded. "She is recovering, but she needs food and rest. I will be right back."

The woman rushed away, but Akari knew she wouldn't be gone for long.

"Sera-sensei," Akari said. "I don't have long. I know they will make me leave you so you can rest. If you need to tell me anything else, now is the time!"

Sera shook her head, but only barely. "You have everything you need now. There is nothing more I can give you...teach you..."

"I'm still your student," Akari said, her eyes brimming with tears. "I need you to guide me."

Sera just shook her head again. The healer came back, along with a few more, and a bowl of broth. They jostled Akari out of the way as they tried to lift Sera's head and make her drink the liquid.

"Please," one of the healers said. She tugged on Akari's arm. "We know what we are doing. Please let us work."

Akari nodded and slowly exited the room. She would have to let the healers do whatever they could to save Sera's life.

And Akari would have to do whatever she could to save the world.

*A*kari went to the hut where Takeo was supposed to be relaxing. When she walked in, she saw a young healer woman sitting at his feet, tending to his ankle. She couldn't suppress the flare of jealousy that coursed through her in that moment.

"Akari," he said with a smile when he saw her. "Vanya-san was just telling me that my ankle has completely healed."

Vanya collected her things and stood, giving Takeo and Akari a respectful bow on her way out. Nothing in her bearing or demeanor indicated she had any interest in Takeo beyond helping his foot. Akari knew her sudden spark of jealousy said more about her own feelings for Takeo than anything about Vanya. She did her best to shake the feeling away as she moved to sit by him.

"That's good," she finally managed to say.

"What's wrong?" he asked, putting his arm around her.

"Nothing," Akari said, shaking her head. "Well, everything, obviously. The goddess ending the world. My sister missing. My lack of ideas of what to do next. But nothing you didn't already know."

He chuckled and kissed her forehead. "Yeah, I know. I guess I meant anything new? How is Sera-san?"

"She is good. Recovering," Akari said. "She woke up for a moment. But then the healers ushered me out, so they could give her some broth and help her rest."

Takeo squeezed her shoulders. "That is *good*, Akari," he said, squeezing her shoulders. "Take the win. You need it."

She nodded and stood up, pacing the room. "I asked her what I should do next. How to find Chiyoko before she grows too powerful. She said I had everything I need. But what could she mean by that? All I have is the sword and the map."

"You also have me," he said, standing up and moving over to a table. "Come here. Let's look at the map together."

Akari sighed, laying it out on the table. "I've already looked at the map a hundred times, from a hundred angles. We found the temple and the cave. There is nothing else on it."

Takeo sighed and leaned over it. "Just let me look."

Akari crossed her arms, waiting for him to admit she was right.

"Did you notice this isn't just a map of the mountain?" he said instead. "It is a map of the whole prefecture."

"Sure," Akari said. "Here is Nasu, Sera's dojo, Kuji village, the coast..."

"Do you have a pen?" he asked. She searched the room and found a pen on another table. "Here is Yahakami village, where the chief's wife went missing." He placed a dot on the map. "And here is Kuji, where Lord Naeran went missing." He placed another dot. "And up here..." He placed a dot on the table up to the north of where it would be if the map showed all of Chiyoko Hollow.

"And here is where the rift was, where the demons poured out when they attacked the city," Akari said, putting her own dot on the map. "And out here is where the ruins are where we found that group of enenra." She placed another dot. "And out here is Hashikami village, where the girl with the birthmark went missing."

"If we look at them," Takeo said. "A pattern emerges."

"My gods," Akari said. "You're right!" The dots all seemed to be spiraling out of a central location. "So if the demons are feeding off Chiyoko's energy, she must be at the center of it all."

"What is this?" Takeo asked, placing his finger right in the center of the dots.

Akari put her hand to her mouth, eyes wide.

"That's my house."

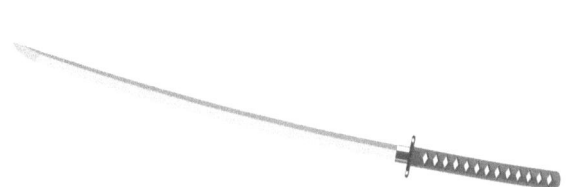

20

*A*kari and Takeo rushed from the building and found Galen.

"We know where Chiyoko was buried," Akari said hurriedly. "We need to go back to Nasu and stop her before she grows too strong."

"How can we help?" Galen asked.

"Just stay here," she said. "Hide. I don't believe I will succeed, but I have to try. Maybe I can at least injure her or distract her or something. Maybe you can strengthen your veil enough to even hide from her."

Galen pressed his lips and looked at Takeo. "There must be more we can do," Galen said. "We cannot hide from a fae goddess. We must be able to help you in some way."

"Then..." Akari was anxious to get back home and didn't have time to put his fears to rest. "Just take care of Sera-sensei. If her strength returns, maybe she can help."

Galen bowed. "We will do what we can," he said.

Akari thought she saw him send a knowing glance of some

sort to Takeo, but she didn't want to try to parse that out right now. She took Takeo's hand.

"You can run us back to Nasu faster than we can ride," she said.

Takeo nodded. Together, they were back in Nasu only minutes later.

Akari went to the dojo first, where she thought the remaining Sword Kissed would probably be. They were there, doing what they could to help the injured. Akari did her best to catch them up on the situation.

"You think Chiyoko is buried under your house?" Kaya asked.

"I don't know," Akari said. "But it's the only theory we have right now."

"I have a theory of my own," Kaya said. She reached into her pocket, pulling out what looked like a page ripped from an old book. "I went to the archives. I searched and searched for anything that might help us. This is the only thing I found."

Akari looked at the paper, and her eyes went wide. On it, there was a drawing of Chiyoko in flowing robes surrounded by cherry blossoms. Of course, Chiyoko looked exactly like Akari, but the clothing and cherry blossoms told Akari she was looking at Chiyoko and not herself. But what was shocking about the image was the sword Akari had taken from the statue of Chiyoko was sticking out of the drawing at Chiyoko's chest.

Chiyoko was dead.

"This...this is all you found?" Akari asked.

Kaya nodded. "There were no words on the pages before or after it. It was in a book, more like an encyclopedia, about the demons and spirits in the world. They all had names and detailed descriptions. This one didn't, though. It terrified me at first because I thought it was a drawing of you."

Akari stared at the image for a minute. She felt almost sick to her stomach, and she knew what Kaya meant. Seeing herself as Chiyoko had been confusing and terrifying. She didn't want to consider what it could mean for her if she and Chiyoko shared more than a face.

Takeo looked over Akari's shoulder at the image. "So if you plunge the sword into the heart of Chiyoko," he said, "you can destroy her."

She felt him squeeze her shoulder. She knew this would give him hope. Hope she could exact revenge on Chiyoko for killing his father. Hope she could destroy the evil that Chiyoko had become.

Hope that she could save the world.

Sakura...sakura...

Akari shrugged his hand off and shook her head. She wasn't sure why she kept hearing that song in the back of her head, or why she felt apprehensive about destroying Chiyoko, but she wasn't going to make her decisions based on some random wordless picture from some old book. If it came down to it, she hoped she would have the strength to do what was necessary. But she also hoped she would have the wisdom to do what was right.

"Come on," Akari finally said, shoving the picture into her pocket along with the map. "Let's get to the house. If we can at least find Yoshimi..."

"We will find her," Kaya said. She then turned to the rest of the Sword Kissed. "Come on, girls. Let's put this bitch back to bed!"

The women all cheered. Akari's heart swelled to have her sisters-in-arms by her side, but she feared for their safety as well. Her Sword Kissed abilities had been useless against Chiyoko until she found Chiyoko's sword. She knew the Sword Kissed would not be able to help her fight, but she also knew that telling them to stay away would be a losing battle. And she didn't need to lose another fight.

Akari, Takeo, and the Sword Kissed all headed toward Akari's house as the sun rose over the village. She had completely lost track of the passage of time over the last couple of days. When had she last slept, or ate? She had no idea. She was at every disadvantage. Was she crazy? She had no business trying to take down a goddess. But as she took in her friends, she realized they were all smiling!

How could they smile at a time like this?

Didn't they know they were all going to die?

Didn't they...

"Akari," Yoshimi yelled.

As they approached what was left of the house, Chiyoko was waiting for them in the garden, under her mother's cherry blossom tree, with Yoshimi wrapped in smoke chains by her side.

"Yoshimi," Akari couldn't help but yell back.

"Get away from here," Yoshimi demanded.

Akari drew her katana. "I can't," she said. "I have to end this."

Chiyoko laughed. "Oh, it will end, Akari. Just not the way you hope."

"Probably not," Akari said, taking a step forward. "But I am here anyway. So let's do this."

Chiyoko laughed again and took a deep breath, sucking in smoke and ash and even some demons into her. She grew big. Her core appeared as if it were made of molten lava.

Akari's heart raced. Takeo and the other Sword Kissed prepared to fight.

Sakura...sakura...

Akari glanced over her shoulder, toward the voice that kept calling her, but as usual, she saw nothing.

"Why are you calling me if you aren't there?" she mumbled. She turned back to Chiyoko and raised her sword, glowing with the power of the Sword Kissed.

Who says I'm not...

For the first time, the voice answered back.

"Who are you?" Akari asked, this time more audibly. Takeo shot her a look, but she ignored him.

I am she...

"She?" Akari asked. "She who?"

Where the nightbloom grow
Is where my heart will find you
She waits there also...

Akari gasped. "She" was Chiyoko. She racked her brain trying to understand what was happening. If the woman speaking to her was Chiyoko and the smoke demon terrorizing the world was also Chiyoko...what did that mean? What was happening?

"Akari," Takeo yelled. "What are you doing? What's wrong? Look!"

Akari turned back to the smoke demon Chiyoko. She was smaller now, breathing hard, as if she was growing angry. But why? She held the advantage. Akari gripped her sword tightly.

Sakura...

A slight breeze blew. Cherry blossoms drifted over her feet and toward Chiyoko.

"S...sakura," Akari called out. Chiyoko froze and narrowed her gaze.

"Sakura! Sakura," Akari yelled again. "Blossoms on the trees, blossoms in the sky..."

Chiyoko screamed at Akari in anger, but she also got a little smaller.

"What is happening?" Takeo asked. Akari had no answer for him, but she kept going.

"Are you a human," she sang, "or are you a fairy? Sakura, sakura of mine..."

Chiyoko took in another deep breath, and even more of the demons flew past their heads as she sucked them in. But even as she sucked in more of the evil, she grew smaller.

"Sakura, sakura," Akari sang again. This time, Takeo joined her.

"Blossoms on the trees, blossoms in the sky," they sang.

Yoshimi twisted and struggled. She broke free and ran to Akari.

"What is happening?" she asked as they embraced.

"I have no idea," Akari said, but she grabbed Takeo's hand and put it on Yoshimi's arm. "Get her out of here!"

He nodded and ran away at full speed, holding Yoshimi's arm tightly.

Akari then took Kaya's hand. "Sing with me," she said.

Kaya nodded to Akari, then to the rest of the Sword Kissed.

> *"Sakura, sakura*
> *Blossoms on the trees*
> *Blossoms in the sky*
> *Are you a human*
> *Or are you a fairy?*
> *Sakura, sakura of mine..."*

They all sang together.

Chiyoko screamed again. She was in so much pain, Akari felt her own heart break for her. Chiyoko continued to suck in the evil, shrinking smaller and smaller until she collapsed.

Everyone stopped singing, confused. Where the demon Chiyoko once stood, threatening them all with death and destruction, there now laid the body of a woman.

"Akari," Kaya said, pushing her toward Chiyoko. "Now is your chance! While she's down!"

Akari stepped up to Chiyoko, but she did not attack. "Chiyoko?" she called.

She couldn't help but gasp when Chiyoko slowly raised her head. Even though she had seen her own face on Chiyoko many times by now, seeing her in a body her own shape and size was jarring.

"Akari..." Chiyoko moaned. She dragged herself up to stand on wobbly legs.

"Chiyoko?" Akari asked.

"It's me," Chiyoko said. "The real me. Rasha's daughter. You called me back...for now. But we don't have much time."

"What do you mean?" Akari asked. "What's going on?"

"As I absorbed the evil, it was as though I was ripped in two," Chiyoko said. "I became two people: myself and the Chiyoko who had absorbed the evil. You called me back, but I am so weak. I cannot...cannot contain her for long."

Chiyoko opened her robe. She revealed that her chest, her heart, was burning like fire.

"Do it, Akari," she said. "Use my sword—our sword—and kill me. Kill her. Destroy the evil that has been plaguing the world."

"No," Akari said. "I can't. You'll die, too!"

"I sacrificed myself for this world centuries ago," Chiyoko said. "And I would do it again and again. I love this world. I begged Mother to bury me here. Do it! Don't let my demon self rise!"

"Do it, Akari," Takeo yelled.

Akari glanced back. He must have come back after getting Yoshimi away.

"I...I can't," Akari said.

"You *can*, Akari," he yelled, screamed, at her. His rage, his need for vengeance, was burning in his eyes. She wanted to alleviate his pain, but there had to be another way.

"If I destroy you," Akari said to Chiyoko, "what about the hollows? The barriers, they protect the world, hold it together. What will happen if I kill you?"

Chiyoko shrunk back for a moment, then shook her head. "I don't know."

They stared at each other, neither sure what to do. But then Chiyoko stood up straight and pulled her robe open wider.

"Do it, Akari! Now," Chiyoko ordered. She began to breathe heavily, and smoke began to coil around her feet. "She's coming back!"

Akari shook her head. She couldn't do it. Not alone. She swiped her sword across her hand, letting her blood flow. She then placed her bleeding hand on Chiyoko's chest.

"Share the burden with me," Akari said. She then screamed, and her head was tossed back as the power, the pain, the darkness coursed through her. But then, the pain stopped, and she felt nothing but pure energy. Pure power. Pure light. She didn't stop absorbing the evil from Chiyoko at half.

She took it all.

She finally stepped back, examining herself. Steam was rising from her body, but no smoke. No darkness. She didn't feel evil.

"What happened?" Akari asked Chiyoko.

"The katana," Chiyoko yelled, pointing.

Akari held it up and saw that it was glowing red hot and throbbing. It was as though a million angry voices were screaming at her from inside the sword. It started to smoke and swell.

"We have to get rid of it," Akari yelled.

"How?" Chiyoko asked.

"Akari! The image from the book," Kaya yelled. "Ram it into her chest and be done with it!"

Akari gazed back at Chiyoko. Chiyoko gave her a smile and placed her hands on Akari's shoulders.

"You have done what you can, Akari-chan," she said. "Thank you." She then kissed Akari on the forehead. She stepped back and opened her robe again. Her face looked serene, at peace with her decision.

Akari stepped back and turned to Takeo.

"Take me to the temple," she ordered.

Realization dawned on his face. Without hesitation, he grabbed Akari's hand and pulled her toward the mountain.

Together, they ran. They ran faster than Akari thought possible. Within seconds, they were at the top of the mountain, at the gate just outside the temple, and Takeo nearly collapsed from exhaustion.

"Go," he panted.

Akari ran to the temple and kicked the door open. She hurried to the statue, and then plunged the sword into Chiyoko's chest.

The statue exploded, blowing Akari out the door and into the yard. The breath was knocked out of her, but as she laid on her back, she saw a beam of black smoke shoot into the sky.

When she could breathe again, Akari sat up. The temple was destroyed, but she was alive, and the evil was gone.

Takeo crawled over to her and put his arms around her.

"You did it, Akari," he said. "You did it."

She put her forehead to his. "I couldn't have done it alone," she said.

He took her face in his hands and placed his lips on hers.

She leaned in and kissed him back. For the first time, she felt free to let go of her fear, her inhibitions, and opened herself up to him completely.

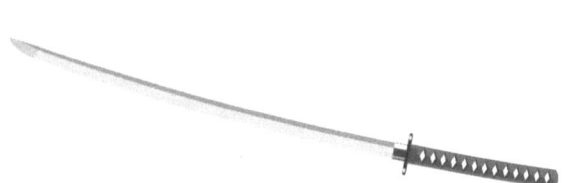

21

*A*kari and Takeo walked back down the mountain hand in hand, but they did not run. The sun was shining, and the hill folk danced around them happily. They knew they needed to get back; everyone would be wondering what happened. But right now, they were at peace, and Akari knew the world was finally safe, finally heading back to some sort of normal. But it would be a long journey. There was still much death and destruction they had to deal with from the days, years, that the earth's evil had been growing.

When they got back to town, Chiyoko and Yoshimi ran to Akari and embraced her.

"You are alive," Yoshimi cried, her eyes brimming with tears. Galen was standing behind her. "Takeo took me to Kuji village, but I couldn't stay there. I had to come back. Galen-ch...san knew I would return on my own if I had to, so he accompanied me."

Akari held her tightly and nodded her head. She then bowed to Galen in thanks.

"Chiyoko's temple is destroyed," Akari said, turning to Chiyoko.

Chiyoko shook her head. "It is fine. It served its purpose."

"Did you know the statue was the key to destroying the evil?" Akari asked.

"I...I don't know," Chiyoko said. "I am so ashamed. I can hardly remember. When Mother buried us, we were terrified. We tried to plan, account for every eventuality, but we had no idea what would happen. And I slept for so long, and then the evil broke free. I can't remember everything. I'm so confused..." She started to cry.

Akari took her into her arms and shushed her. "It will all be okay," Akari said. "The evil is gone now. Everything will be fine."

"Will it?" Yoshimi asked. "The evil rose once...twice, I guess. The first time was when you had to be buried to contain it, and a second time a few days ago. Will it rise again?"

Akari wanted to say no. That the evil had been expelled from the earth forever, but how could she know for sure? What if even one piece remained? Could it once again grow into something beyond what they could control?

She just shook her head. "It is gone for today. Let that be enough for a few hours."

Yoshimi nodded, placing her arm around Chiyoko. Awestruck, she eyed Chiyoko and Akari, laughing. "I'm not sure I can get used to this."

"Oh," Chiyoko said. "I forgot. I haven't seen a mirror in hundreds of years." She ran her hands over herself, fluttering her fingers, and her appearance changed. Her robes were still the old style, but they were no longer black, but pale pink and white and embroidered with sakura flowers. She was taller now. Her hair was piled on her head in a traditional style and her face changed. She was incredibly beautiful. To Akari's relief, she looked like a different person.

"What do you think?" Chiyoko asked.

"Much better," Akari said. "Thank you. I'm not sure I could have handled having the face of a goddess for much longer."

Chiyoko spread her arms and turned her face to the sky, taking in a deep breath. "Oh, to be free," she said.

"What will you do now?" Akari asked.

"I am going to eat," Chiyoko said. "I'm starving. Then I am going to go to the mountains for a while to meditate. Re-center myself. Make sure there is no evil left in me and learn myself again."

"I wouldn't mind finding something to eat myself," Akari said.

"And then, I will return," Chiyoko said. "I have been awake for a very short while, but even I can see the rifts that still exist in this world."

"What do you mean?" Yoshimi asked.

"Where are my lovely fae?" Chiyoko asked. "Other than Takeo and Galen, there are no fae here. Where are they?"

"They live apart from humans," Akari admitted. "In their own villages."

"That cannot do," Chiyoko said. "Humans and fae are meant to share this world."

"What about the fae realm?" Takeo asked. "What happened to it?"

Chiyoko nodded. "It is safe," she said. "It is protected from this world. When we created the hollows, we sealed the fae realm away completely, along with everyone who was in it at the time, fae and human. But that is something we need to work on as well. If we can find a way to remove the divides that separate the hollows, we can hopefully find a way back to the fae lands as well."

Takeo exhaled in relief and nodded his head, clearly overcome with emotion. "That would be wonderful, my lady. Truly wonderful."

Akari held tight to Chiyoko's hands, not wanting to let her go just yet. Over Chiyoko's shoulder, she saw Malia, Galen's maid, one of Sera's healers, and some of the other Kuji fae coming toward her. She took Chiyoko with her to greet them.

"This is Chiyoko," Akari said. "We were able to purge the evil out of her."

"We saw the explosion, Akari-san," Malia said. "And when we didn't all die, we thought you must have been successful." She, and the rest of the fae, all bowed to Chiyoko. "We are humbled to meet you, our lady."

She placed her hands on her shoulders and raised her up. "And I am honored to meet you and to start healing the wounds of this land."

"I should go to Kuji," Akari said. "I want to see Sera and tell her what happened. And find out what else she knows."

The healer's face turned solemn, and she handed a piece of paper to Akari. "I am sorry, Akari-san," she said. "She passed away not long after you left Kuji. But not before she had me write this."

"What?" Akari asked, too shocked to take the paper from her. "She...she's gone?"

Yoshimi put her arms around her sister. "I'm so sorry, imouto," she said.

With trembling fingers, Akari finally let the healer place the paper in her hand. She opened it slowly.

Akari,

I am sorry I must leave you now. I know you will find some way to succeed. You are not just Sword Kissed, but the light of Chiyoko herself. I leave you my dojo, so you may train the next generation of Sword Kissed. Even if you banish the evil, the world will always need protectors. I can think of no one better to replace me than you.

Good luck, Akari-chan. I mean, Akari-sensei.

"She...she left me the dojo," Akari said. "She wants...wanted me to be the new sensei for the Sword Kissed."

She felt Takeo's hand on her shoulder. He undoubtedly

remembered what she had told him about not wanting to be a Sword Kissed at all. Not wanting to train the future Sword Kissed.

About not choosing this life.

"What are you going to do?" he asked.

Akari folded the paper and held it to her chest. Somehow, Sera knew her better than she knew herself. When Akari wanted to give up, Sera wouldn't let her. And when Akari didn't know what path her future would take, Sera did.

Sera knew Akari would always choose the Sword Kissed.

"I will accept," Akari said. "I am Sword Kissed. I am the descendant of Chiyoko. I am the Light. What else could I do?"

"But is it what you want?" he asked. "Will it give you purpose?"

"My people, all of them—fae and human—are my purpose," she said.

She didn't know what the future would hold, but she knew that as long as she had Yoshimi, Chiyoko, and Takeo by her side, they would have hope.

They would save the world together.

THANK YOU

I hope you enjoyed SWORD KISSED. If you did, please consider
leaving a review on
AMAZON

http://amzn.to/2G4s6F5

and GOODREADS.

https://www.goodreads.com/book/show/35714495-sword-kissed

Don't forget to check out the rest of the books in the DARK FAE
HOLLOWS series at
CharmedLegacy.com

When Ethan discovers that the love of his life, Victoria, is actually the child of a monstrous beast and must marry another man to save her family, he retreats to a monastery to live out the rest of his days alone.

But the Church has other ideas.

Ethan's mentor asks him to lead famous vampire hunter Dom Calmet back to his home village to rid the town of the vampires that plague it. Ethan must then take a journey, emotionally and literally, back to the town of his youth and decide between love and faith when he once again meets The Vampire's Daughter.

Containing many tropes of a classic Gothic novel (an obscure heroine, an indecisive hero, an exotic location, references to classical literature, dark castles, a foreboding sense of danger) combined with the sensuality of a modern romance, The Vampire's Daughter will leave you gasping for more.

AMAZON: http://amzn.to/2DreqlT

Once upon a time, a vampire and a witch fell in love, and that love fractured the world. Now divided into sixteen isolated Divisions, the world is an unstable and dangerous place.

In the Division of NOLA, Catheryn Beauregard fears her burgeoning magical powers. Hiding as just another slave in the home of the Hoodoo Queen, Catheryn hopes her simplistic powers will simply go unnoticed. And her plan seems to be working...until the Hoodoo House is attacked by a ruthless band of vampire pirates.

Captain Rainier Dulocke and his crew need humans to feed on. In an act of desperation, they beset the Hoodoo House and take ten slaves to sustain them. Rainier takes a girl named Catheryn for himself, but her blood is giving him terrible side effects. Still, he refuses to give her up. Even when the Hoodoo Queen demands her return.

The NOLA Division is in danger. The waters are rising. Food is running out. And the Hoodoo Queen is about to destroy everything that's left if the pirates don't meet her request. Now Catheryn must choose who will die: the humans who sold her, the witches who bought her, or the vampires who stole her. If she fails to decide, everyone could die.

AMAZON: http://amzn.to/2BMjel3

ABOUT THE AUTHOR

Leigh Anderson loves all things Gothic and paranormal. She did her master's thesis on vampire imagery in Gothic novels and met her husband while assuming the role of a vampire online. She currently teaches writing at several universities and has a rather impressive collection of tiny hats. She lives in a small town in the mountains where she raises bearded dragons and gives them wings for Halloween. She is currently working on too many writing projects, and yet not enough.

Sign up for her mailing list and stalk her around the web to keep in touch and be the first to learn about new releases.

Newsletter: http://leighandersonromance.com/subscribe/
Facebook: https://www.facebook.com/LeighAndersonRomance/
Twitter: https://twitter.com/LeighA_Romance/
Goodreads: https://www.goodreads.com/leighanderson
Amazon: http://amzn.to/2wAo2t9
Bookbub: https://www.bookbub.com/authors/leigh-anderson-755d218b-1d7b-4aa2-97f9-427cb3c12f98
Instagram: https://www.instagram.com/shreddedpotatoart/
Google+: https://plus.google.com/u/0/+LeighAndersonRomance/

www.ingramcontent.com/pod-product-compliance
Lightning Source LLC
Chambersburg PA
CBHW031127210626
46816CB00015B/1067